BEYOND

THE

TOWER

Book 1 of The Journey Series

Beyond the Tower

JacQueline Vaughn Roe

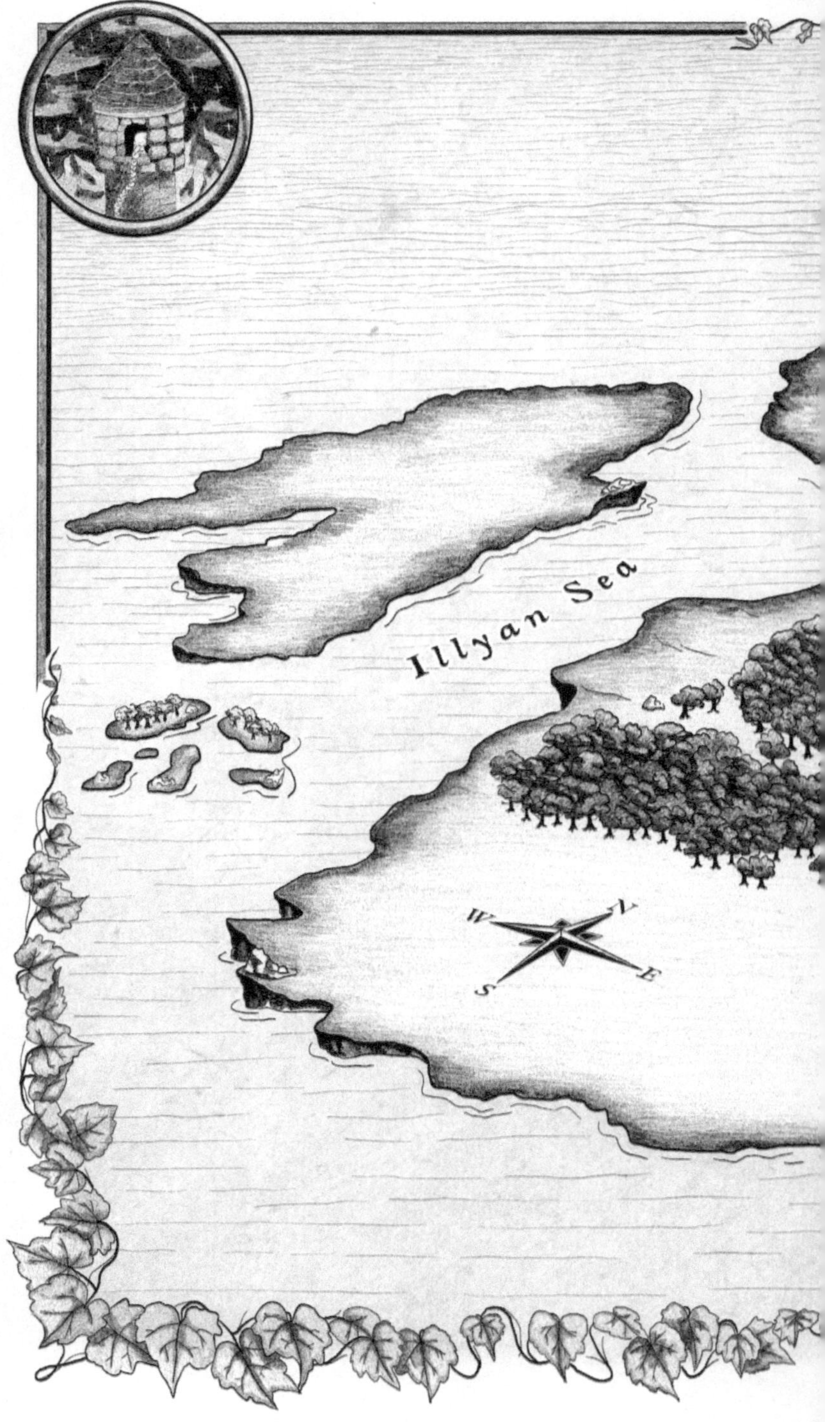

Illyan Sea
W N E S

DOONTRISSE-MOUNTAINS
Rapunzel's Tower
Veritas River
Dorothea's Cottage
Bluebeard's Fortress
Convent
Auriel River
Helga's Cottage
THE DARK WOOD
ALLERIA

CONTENTS

SUNFLOWERS

She's cut them down.

I am lying in a field, the fragrance of sun-heated grass and crushed flowers hitting me as I raise my head. I slowly lift myself to see the carnage. Giant brown sunflower heads lay decapitated all around me, their green stalks sticking up every which way with bright golden petals strewn about.

I close my eyes, hoping this is a dream. It must be a dream. I am not here, surely he is still coming for me—but when I open my eyes, all I see is the wreck of the field of sunflowers. My head throbs where she yanked my hair. I reach back and feel the shorn, bristling mass it is now.

Why?

She says I betrayed her.

EVERY MORNING THIS SUMMER, I woke up and looked out to see them growing at the base of the square wall that enclosed my tower. Their great yellow and brown heads bobbed in the wind, nodding good morning to me.

They gave the wall color, texture, a reminder that something lay beyond it, waiting for me to rise and leave the tower.

But now she's cut them down. Now she's cut *me* down and I know she'll never let me be with him again.

◌⟨℘⟩◌

MOST DAYS I would walk the circle of my chamber and read. The curved wall stretching from the left side of my bed to the window was filled with a rounded bookcase encompassing every piece of literature she deemed worthy of my mind. She also allowed me some stories I think she thought too fanciful and romantic, but she indulged me— resting, I believe, in the knowledge that I was safe from trying out any of the ideas they might have inspired in me.

I should have known. I suppose I did know . . .

I loved my books. I read many over and again, but I always felt listless when I put one away to reach for another. Books are meant to be enjoyed, not to be the whole of one's existence. I suppose she wanted to be that: the whole of my existence. Perhaps I simply existed to please her and I did, until now.

From the right side of my bed to the window, I created a living area with a table and two chairs, cupboard next to the hooded fireplace, cauldron hanging ready. I never lacked for fresh food, water, or wood; by magic they appeared every morning and I set about my chores. I suppose I should be grateful to her for that, but eating well within a prison does not make one less a prisoner.

Each day I cleaned my dishes, the black cauldron, and swept out the ashes and dirt to the ground below my window. She never minded the mess it made, simply brushed it to the side when she called for my rope of hair. I kept the tower tidy, my clothes clean, our meals flavorful, our conversation interesting. But I missed gardening, I missed running, I missed hearing people. As the days passed and I gazed out beyond my tower's window, I wondered what it would be like to live outside her protection.

THIS THOUGHT WAS NOT NEW. I think it was the reason I came to live in my tower, but I always stuffed the it down, imagining it crumpling smaller and smaller until it disappeared. But that was wrong—the desire swelled and took over. My ordinary life changed forever late one night.

THE DAY HAD SMACKED of normality, full of routine and monotonous waiting, as usual. Her visits had become erratic, her voice was rough like the bark of a tree when she told me she would visit when she could. I tried not to ask for more, though the longing to share my life with someone grew within me.

I had a feeling she was coming, an inkling that something was on its way. All that week I had stood at my window every night to sing—but for the first time, I had heard something. Was something calling me? Was it time for me to find my way outside her grasp? I tried to snuff out the thought like I would put out my candle each night, depriving the flame of the air it needed to breathe, making it sputter and die. If I just left this thought alone, it would suffocate. But I caught myself standing and singing and listening longer each night. I wanted something to happen.

As I went about my chores, I dreamed of the things we used to plant in her garden, things I wanted to plant at the base of my tower, things I would harvest if I were allowed to leave. I wondered, if I could create a world beyond that wall, what would it look like? Would it hate me, as she says it does, turn me ugly like her? Or could she be wrong?

When she came at the end of my long day of dreaming and snuffing out thoughts, she looked into my face and told me a tale as she sat before the fire, rocking. Her shining eyes lingered on the flames, her bony, veined hands stroking the worn wood of the rocking chair's arms. Her wispy white hair stuck out at odd angles. She never smoothed it or attempted to modify her appearance. I saw her notice me watching her, and she grinned, revealing her perfect teeth inside a shriveled mouth.

Her story changed and shifted as she spoke. I questioned what was true—I thought I could remember life before my tower—but perhaps that was just one of her stories. Did I ever live outside?

In this tale, there was a woman, just one this time, who was hungry and craving a treat. She was round and could not get it herself, so she sent her husband to steal for her. He did, time and again, as he preferred to debase himself and those from whom he stole, rather than deprive his wife. The witch watched him for a time.

"But I caught him there, in my garden." Her eyes grew bright recalling. "How quick he was to sink to his knees! How fast he was to cry out 'Mercy!'—he who would have called out for my burning if he had but had a crowd with him.

"The world of men is strange. They cannot stand on their own, they cannot live by themselves as I have. No! They must have one another to feel strong, for they must scream together to make a roar instead of a whine.

"But he had no one with him, and so he whined. He promised me anything, and I felt pity for him. I let him go."

"What did he promise you?" My words were as soft as petals, dropping to my stone floor.

Her eyes shrank. "A trifle to him, the world to me." And she was soon gone, down my hair and into the world as always. She left me behind again, watching the sunlight fade on the horizon. I waited for the moon to keep her vigil, though she was waning, and in a few nights' time I would be all alone to guard the night in my tower.

CAPTIVE

It tied me there, it kept me there—I was the way to get out, I was the way to get in. I was the only door to my tower, my hair from the lone window. She came when she wished and she exited, forsaking me, *protecting me*, she said—always protecting me.

"From what," I once asked her, "from sunflowers and sunshine?" "No," her eyes flashed, "from the world of men! I'm protecting you from who they are and what they'll do."

As I stand over the slain bodies of my sunflowers, I think of her answer and the tale that had followed. It was a different one, of cruel men, and her rusty voice rose and fell, recounting her life's triumphs and agonies.

She was a child once, this monster, this ogress, my best friend and captor. She was a child, beautiful and innocent as children are; she was loud and rowdy as all have been. Walking to the market one day, she met her fate: an old woman crossing the road. Her childish face must have wrinkled at the smell of the woman, because the old woman turned and cursed her. "You think you smell better, little brat? You think you're a beauty? It will be your curse! All you long for you will never be able to hold, all you reach for will be taken from you. You will die alone and lonely. All your birds will have wings and they will leave you crippled. Mark my words, child."

She ran home to her mother and sobbed. Together, they went straight to the priest. She confessed all her evil thoughts, all she could think to confess, but the curse stuck like a splinter in her mind, whittling away her peace.

"I was alone from that day forward, for no one trusted me. I grew strange. I grew different from others. I was fascinated by my solitude, consumed by it." She spoke in bitterness, little prickles having multiplied through the years.

I remember how I could not look away from her, and she read my thoughts.

"When did I lose my beauty? When do all witches lose their beauty . . .? When they gain their power. I am still lovely, but a woman with power *must* be hideous to look at, so I mask my looks. It keeps the world of men away."

She is odd. What else had they done to her to make her hate them? One curse could not have caused the mutation of a handsome child into a witch—could it?

"Why do you hate them so?"

"If you knew them, you would know."

"For me to know them, you would have to let me go."

She laughed her raspy laugh—"And that I never will!"—then stroked my long golden braid which she had spread over her lap. Her teeth showed when she laughed;

they were white and straight, reminding me that somewhere inside her hides that beautiful, twisted child.

"Do you miss your life from before?" It was a simple
question, and I was not being impertinent by asking it. "Do
you?" Something happened; something began to transform
her appearance for a moment. But it was just a moment,
and though I recall it as I stand here among the ruins of
my life, I know that I will never witness what was trying to
emerge. Not unless she wants me to. It only now occurs to
me that she was a captive, too.

⟡

I REMEMBER LYING down one night after standing and
singing out into the inky darkness, but I found I couldn't
sleep. I stood up and resumed my place by the window,
restless. I was tired of my life, of my patterns of reading
and writing. I knew I could not find the peace in my solitude that she claimed to have found in hers—I needed
something more.

I heard it again. There was a soft thud and more movement, closer. I tried to speak, but though my mouth
opened, the words were frozen inside my lungs and I could
not breathe.

She began calling my name. Why would she do that, I
wondered. She had already come earlier that evening. I
anchored my braid, dropped the rest down, and waited for
her to climb.

"Rapunzel." Her voice was too deep, and I reached for
the candle I had lit and placed on the table.

I should have been terrified, I should have screamed or

run or called out for help. But instead, I reached out my hand to touch the man coming in my window.

"Who are you?" I gaped. He was so tall, and his face was broader than my witch's, with a red tint to his weathered skin. He seemed much younger than my witch but older than I; the hazel eyes looked at me curiously beneath thick, dark brown eyebrows under his headdress, a headdress of wrapped green liripipe which covered him from crown to just below his shoulders. His lips were full, and he was moving towards me with soundless footsteps, as though approaching a frightened animal.

"Just a man. My name is Paul." He was staring, too. "Is your name Rapunzel?"

"Yes." I put down the candle and tried to focus my thoughts as I went to sit down on the opposite side of the table—and, too late, remembered that I was still anchored to the wall. Although I'm sure I looked comical, the man was very kind, helping me regain my footing and gather my hair.

"Are you all right?" His green tunic was much shorter than mine, with close-fitted leggings underneath them. So unused to the appearance of legs, it took me a moment before I realized I was gawking.

I removed my hand with haste from his and tried to smile as I rubbed my head. "Yes, I suppose you just startled me."

"I'm sorry, I knew of no other way to meet you."

"There is no other way."

He continued gazing at me, and I found I was becoming uncomfortable. "How long have you been here?" I suppose he smiled to set me at ease.

"I don't know. I've tried to guess—it must be close to six or seven years."

"Do you never get out?"

"Only in my head." His quick glance made me question if I'd said something inappropriate.

He turned to take in my spacious chamber, his astonished eyes dwelling on my stuffed bookcase. "You read?"

"Of course. It—" He looked at me with those unblinking eyes, and I had to walk away from him, over to the bookcase with my hair snaking behind me. "—it helps me."

"But not tonight."

I didn't know what to say to that, so I just reached for a book and opened its soft leather cover without seeing anything.

I knew he wanted to say more, wanted to know more, but he seemed to sense my discomfort.

"May I come again?" He waited as I anchored my braid again.

"I don't know." I forced myself to take a breath, still trying to look up at him.

"If you want me to, just let down your hair; if not, don't, and I won't come again." Saying only this, he departed as he came, in quiet movements.

THE TREE

I feel the tears wetting my face now as I think of that first night together. We didn't know each other yet—could I have saved him? I remember wondering, would she know when she looked at me? Would she feel that I had betrayed her? What would she have had me do? Perhaps I should have pushed him out the window once I saw his face—of course, he might have grabbed me and we both would have ended at the bottom of the tower. Would she have liked that?

After he left, I fell into a tangle of dreams, the kind from which one wakes feeling distressed, but uncertain of what happened. The following morning I determined that if he came again, I would already be sleeping. That way, he would leave and I could be as innocent as possible. By midmorning my resolve diminished, and I found myself thinking of my childhood while I was kneading bread. It was as though my mind began turning back the pages of memories, evaluating what had once been so that I could determine what should come next.

Before I lived in my tower, the witch and I lived together in her house. It was not a circle or square, but a cozy wooden dwelling with a thatched roof. It contained one great room in which we did our living, cooking, and eating, and a loft in which we did our sleeping. I remember walking around and singing, being quiet when she was gone so that I could hear more of the people that scuffled by outside her garden walls. It was hard to understand them as they spoke in soft tones. The best part about being in the garden was that I could hear something of them, I could hear them moving, and I could hear children laughing. I remember laughing myself, wanting to join them, to share in their joys and trials, their journeys.

My mind was always flitting from one question to another as I listened, trying to imagine their lives outside her walls. What was a priest, and why must the girls confess to him? What sort of god was he that, though they confessed, he could not remove a young girl's curse? The boys passing by sounded rude, daring each other to spit on her walls, daring each other to enter, to steal something. None of them did, though—they spoke of her many eyes.

She was so funny when she chanced to overhear them and would make faces imitating their slander. She would make me giggle, and then things would grow silent except for faster footfalls.

One day there was a strange cry. I could not have been more than six or seven. It was a man's voice. "Please, let me see her—" It was all I heard before she whisked me inside, locking me in from the outside. I ran to the lowest window, throwing open the shutter. I watched in fascination as she went to the wall, her harsh voice rising to silence the voice on the other side. Then she was gone for hours, reappearing later as though nothing had happened.

Her garden wall had no door; she needed none, though I never asked how she got in and out.

When she looked at me after that, her gaze held an odd expression. The older I got, the more anxious she seemed. During those young years, she had taught me how to read and write, to sew and embroider, to garden and cook. In the garden was every kind of vegetable, rows of red and green cabbages, soft spinach and peppery arugula. Some rows seemed to have nothing, but she smiled and taught me what grew beneath the surface: parsnips, carrots, onions, potatoes, even ginger. There were mounds of squash, and I loved to stroke their rough, bumpy surfaces. Best of all was the herb garden right next to the tomato plants. When the summer sun would heat the air, the pungent smell of the tomatoes would mingle with the basil and rosemary. She taught me to run and play, and I would dash between the rows feeling free, until I would come up against a wall. Each row ended with the towering wall, standing guard and looking down at me. It was an ever-present reminder that I must always stay inside.

In an open area to the north of the massive garden, there was one tree that I learned to climb when she wasn't looking. I remember thinking I could go higher and higher and touch the sky. I didn't look out to see our neighbors at first, but then I recognized my proximity to others. There was a house a little way away, and a road of some sort. The tree was far enough away from the wall that, though I could see beyond my home, it could not help me get out. But I learned what I could from it.

When I was eleven, I became overwhelmed with the need to see more, so I climbed whenever I got the chance. It was seldom that she wasn't watching me now. Her every move seemed fretful. Then some dam within her broke, and she was gone with increasing frequency. I was happy to sit in my tree and dream of being outside without ever worrying about the reality of traveling there.

One day, I saw a dark-haired boy who kept passing by. Not many days later, he noticed me and smiled. I had become quite bold at this age, ogling and forgetting to hide. Though we never spoke, something in me twittered each time he walked by. I wanted to know his name; I wanted to see what color his eyes were. I wanted something outside her walls.

She knew it and swooped down to take me to my tower. She was outraged; I remember how scared I was. I cried and begged her to forgive me. I realize now that my tower was not a punishment; it was something she had been planning, something she had been building. It was not finished when she brought me. It seems that even her magic has limitations, but she guarded me until she could place me inside.

The memory of my childhood had its way with me. I could see, as I stood there forming the stretchy dough into shape, what she had done to me. She never needed me to come into the tower, but she used my hair to remind me that I would stay there by myself without a way of escape. I made up my mind: I became determined to have a friend outside of her. I could only guess that was what he could become, but he was my one chance to know if such a thing could exist.

As I set about my other chores, waiting for her to come, I wondered if she would sense my turmoil and guess my scheme.

15

THE MIST

She came that night with seeds. She'd harvested some of the sunflowers and told me to break the shell with my teeth and eat the meat inside. I did, all the while questioning if I was betraying myself while she talked. I loved the flowers; they gave color to my world. But the meat sustained me as I listened to another tale.

In this one, many women were on their way into the village. They walked past her garden wall and found themselves enclosed in a mist.

"Did you make the mist?" I asked.

"No, their desires did. People long for things they cannot name, they long for the power they do not trust. I was confirmed with some of those women . . ." She contemplated before continuing. "There was one among them; she was the youngest and her yearning was the greatest. They trespassed and walked beyond my wall. They gathered what was not theirs. But this did not satisfy her, and her craving became greater than ever before. She came again in secret, alone this time; her greed had made her bold. She came many times to take what she did not own." She lapsed into silence while she sucked on the salty shell, then she split it with her teeth and spit it out into a wooden bowl.

"Did you see her?"

She looked up as she bit into the meat. "I knew her well. I knew her quite well. When she came, I would hide and watch. She grew careless, and the rounder she got, the more clumsy and reckless she became. She thought she had a right to what was not hers."

"What happened to her?"

"A tiger ate her." She smiled, revealing her beautiful teeth beyond her snarled lips.

⸎

I FELT strange letting down my hair for someone other than my witch. Part of me had doubted if he existed or if my mind had concocted him out of all the stories I had read. Dangerous things, stories—they give the mind all sorts of ideas on how life should be, how life can be. I found myself searching to find it, the life beyond my tower.

His eyes were such happy things—sharp, intuitive, kind, green or brown?—but I told myself I should not be quick to trust, since many women have been lowered to their disastrous fate by trusting too easily.

"Why have you come?" I was in earnest.

"To see if you would allow me inside." His words came without hesitation as he freed my braid and then drew the rest of it inside.

"Thank you." I tried not to be distracted by him, but it

was odd having him there, seeing someone so tall, someone who smelled of musk and sunshine. "But why did you come in the beginning?"

He turned and smiled at me, his eyes wrinkled in the corners as though a pleasant memory was warming him. "I heard a voice." He waited until I wound my hair back through the room so that neither of us would trip on it, and then we both sat at my table where I poured us tea that I had ready . . . in hopes he was real.

"What do you mean, you heard a voice?"

One large hand cupped the mug and he cooled it with his breath before taking a sip and then telling his story. "My mare and I were out hunting, and I followed a buck farther into the wood than I had ever been before. A mist rose at dusk and I realized, too late, I had lost my way. The buck had fallen in the bright yellow field of flowers beside the wall and your tower. As I gathered the buck to carry it back, I heard a voice. Your—your captor was leaving by a disappearing rope, and I hid so that she would not see me. But I heard you singing after she had gone, and I found myself determined to meet you. As you know, the wall has no door, your tower no ladder, but I knew that I must return to find the secret of her entrance."

"How did you find your way home?"

His smile was confident, though not with arrogance. "I am a hunter and I have an excellent horse. It was not easy, but with patience I found it."

"How long until you could find me again?" My fingers fidgeted in my lap, pinching the lavender material of my outer dress, the surcoat.

"A week." He looked confused. "Though I searched

and searched, everything that seemed familiar led me astray. At last, I closed my eyes and blindfolded my horse."

"You found the mist again, and it led you?"

"Eventually." I had known why no one had ever ventured near, since the witch boasted of her spell over the field of flowers. "I found them again, and then the wall and your tower. I had to know who you were; I needed to hear you again. I listened to you once more, then returned last night. Once I saw the old woman leave I couldn't wait any longer. I scaled the wall to meet you."

"Now you know." I observed him, questioning what more he could want, questioning what I wanted.

"Not enough," he smiled, and I felt something tickle within me.

I took a deep breath to calm myself, to make the odd feeling go stale. "She will punish you if she finds you here."

"And you?"

I slowly shook my head and then willed myself to speak. "I don't know."

"Then why did you let me inside again?"

"I don't know."

"Were you curious?"

I nodded. "I still am." I looked around my room. "I want to know more than my books can tell me, I want to know more than her stories say."

"Why has she put you here?" His question seemed out of his mouth before he could find a better way to phrase it.

"She says it is to protect me. I think it is because she is scared."

I blink; I don't want to remember any more. I step carefully over the carcasses littering the field. I cannot see my wall or my tower. I can see nothing but ravaged flowers in all directions around me. It feels odd to be on the ground, to be able to walk around. My stomach rumbles, but I can't tell what time of day it is. The sky above is a bright shining surface, painful to look at, without a single sun. I am in a place of her making. The witch has sent me here to remember I made a mistake in betraying her, but all I can do is remember that I was not clever enough to escape her grasp with Paul. I shake my head and feel the silent tears coursing down my cheeks. I cannot stop them any more than I can stop remembering.

⌘

His visits were more consistent than hers. I came to count on them as I did breathing. Each time I saw her coming I knew he was behind her, and I did all I could to act as I always did, tried to not hurry the visit along so that she would never suspect who was at her heels. But I longed for her to go, I longed for her to leave so that he would climb up to me and tell me more, teach me more. I longed for things I did not understand, but I wanted them, I wanted things to happen, I wanted the night to last forever, for it to cloak me in its dark arms and gather me away from my tower so that she would never find me, never keep me from him a moment longer.

The books call this love, though she calls it greed. I am unsure of what it is except that it is all-consuming. There was a night he did not come and I found myself crying with shame. Had he left to never return? What had I said or done to upset him?

When he returned the following evening, he explained that his absence could not be helped. His large hands, when uncovered by riding gloves, had thick blunt fingers, and he used them to show his regret as he spoke. He spread them out then, palms up, showing his helplessness, but all I could see was their strength, a strength I should not trust. I heard my cool voice reply that though I appreciated his visits, he need not concern himself with apologies. I would be happy to see him if he desired, but I could do just as well without him.

"I'm sorry you feel that way." He turned to leave, which was impossible without my help.

"Why are you leaving, sir?" I continued in my distant tone, trying to understand why my throat was swelling and irritating tears were again filling my eyes.

"Because, my lady, I would hate to inconvenience you or waste your time. I had thought you enjoyed these evenings as did I and felt the rest of the day a nuisance waiting for night to approach so that we could be together again." He turned to look at me with hot anger in his bright hazel eyes.

I could not stop the pesky tears from soaking my face, so I turned from him, but not before he had seen.

"I would not have missed last evening if it could have been helped." His voice was soft and he placed those two strong hands on my shoulders. I struggled to breathe as he turned me to face him.

"Then why did you not tell me the evening before?"

"I didn't know, but I'll do my best never to let it happen

again." He pulled me to him and I felt my body shudder, though it was confusing as to why I would react in such a manner. His nearness overwhelmed me and I tried to calm down.

My dreams that night left me mystified. In them, he kept holding me, touching my face, kissing my lips. I had read of kissing once in a book and thought it sounded strange. Of course, I no longer have that book; my witch was incensed when she discovered it and snatched it away muttering something about those who work against her. She never explained, and I never asked. Before she took it, though, I had memorized the more confusing words of the scene, and I wondered what it would be like if he did lower his face to mine and seal my lips with a kiss. If they were sealed, would I no longer be able to speak? Why would he do that? Why did I want him to?

SUSPICIONS

By this time, she was suspicious. She knew something was different about me. I could tell by the way she looked at me from then on, the way she came earlier, more often, and began working to create a garden as I had once asked her to do. With her sorcery, she made roses bloom all around the base of the tower, but I found myself still gazing at the sunflowers beyond the wall —the sunflowers that led Paul to me.

The witch brought a calico cat to me. Lovely Cat purred in my lap, nudging me to stroke her black-brown-white fur until I did. She became mischievous and played with my hair. I laughed at Cat and thanked the witch for her kindness.

She looked at me and said that she knew I was lonely and was doing her part to relieve it. I didn't feel as grateful as perhaps I should have; I knew that she would never release me, that my loneliness was due to her warped perceptions.

Her stories changed again, she told me more of the

harshness of the world of men. I tried to fathom again what had happened to cause her to feel this way.

She left after twisting her tales about me, and I resumed waiting. Something was unraveling, something was shifting. I worried that meant that Paul would not come to me, but I heard him at last—and within a few moments he entered my world, bringing his own to me.

I didn't know what I was doing, but it was as though I was avoiding Paul. My desire mounted and I traveled about the room wrapping up my hair as I did every night, but something was different.

"What's wrong?"

"Nothing is wrong," I said in a choked voice, careful not to trip over Cat who sprang up onto the bed and looked at my soggy eyes with curiosity.

"Then why won't you look at me?" I looked up to see him smiling and I found myself approaching him. I lifted my chin and he saw what I'd been avoiding, what I'd been hoping for.

He leaned down and his lips touched mine, sending chills throughout my being. I kissed him back and at last I understood why someone would want to be kissed.

"I love you." It was out of my mouth and traveling towards his ears before I realized I'd said it.

"Then let me take you away. Come with me now." His words were hungry, his meaning clear.

I gazed at him, unsure of what should happen next. "How?"

All at once, he looked distressed, throwing a glance out into the night. "I left it"—he muttered an oath—"after riding out with it almost every time I've come, I left my rope with our stable-hand. He needed something stronger than what he had, but if I had known—"

I placed my trembling fingers to his lips to stop the regrets.

"I swear to you, I will bring a rope tomorrow if you like and we will go away from this place."

"And then what?" I felt like a child, thrilled and mystified.

"Let me marry you."

I know what marriage is: it is where you are willing to sacrifice yourself so that your spouse won't be denied. The best marriages happen when both are willing to do this, or so I have read. "I don't know . . ." I started to say, but his lips were on mine and I felt as though I was on fire. Anything separating us I wanted to be gone, I wanted to be with him forever, living with him forever —*but what if she finds us?* This thought brought a halt to my dream-making. She could cause him to suffer, she would harm him and I would be left knowing I had caused his pain.

I pulled away, "I can't let you—" But I stopped as a wounded look came over his eyes.

"What? Did you think I would hurt you?"

"No, but I can't go with you. She will find us—"

"She's not found us yet. We'll depart tomorrow and she'll never know."

"She will find out and she will find you and . . ."

He shook his head, laughing in his confidence.

Why didn't I argue? Why didn't I insist? I could have saved him, but I was too needy, and I allowed his kisses to change my mind. I was determined I couldn't stay in my tower any longer. Like a fool, I believed him and I thought I could leave her behind.

⌘

THE EVENING THAT FOLLOWED, she brought me another present. All day long I had been unsure as to what I would do when she came, how I should act, how I could conceal the truth, but her generosity shocked me in such a way that I didn't have to worry about it anymore.

"Cats like toys," she smiled. "Is that not true, Cat?"

She leaned over the calico and dangled a rigid, paralyzed mouse by the tail. I excused myself to use the chamber pot so that I would not have to witness the mouse's demise. I heard her laughing before I returned and asked what was amusing.

"Your Cat, she tells me such interesting things, such funny things."

"Oh?"

"Of course, she has told me that you like to sing her to sleep at night."

"I do." I smiled with affection at Cat. "The songs you used to sing to me when I was a child, I sing them at night and now it is nice to sing them to her. Thank you for bringing her to me."

"Of course, I could not have known about your man otherwise."

"What?" I felt as though the tower was moving, swaying to the earth and bringing me down with it. I blinked to steady myself and feigned ignorance at her accusation.

"Your man, the one you've been hiding from me."

I laughed with far more courage than I felt. "How could I hide a man from you? You know every cranny of this tower."

She did not appreciate my wit, and she hissed at me. "The man who comes to see you after I leave each evening. Did you think I wouldn't find out about him?"

"No, of course not."

"Then, why did you not tell me of him yourself?" Her small withered frame stretched tall, her white, frazzled hair a contrast to her reddened face.

I stared at her and felt myself dwindling. What would she do to me? What form of punishment could she have in store for breaking her most sacred rule? "You would have hurt him."

"Would have? Will!" Her appearance shifted, and she shimmered in fury and agony. "Has he dared to touch you? To sully my most precious—" Her tone was a curse to my ears, but I could not shut them as I wished. As I turned from her, she yanked my hair and hacked it from my head. I felt naked, bereft and alone. The small bit of hair I had left was wild.

I heard myself screaming. I didn't know why, but my voice had a will of its own and it kept shrieking. She held out her hands and my voice hiccupped outside my mouth, traveling to her. She pinched it shut and leered at me. I tried to calm myself, and I felt the world around me shrinking, altering. I landed face down on the earth.

◌҉

IN THE MIDDLE of the field of flowers, there suddenly appears a pond with an image reflected on its skin. In the portal, I see my beloved's face as the witch throws him out of the tower into the thorns below. Will I be able to shut out the sound of his howls, of his anguish? I watch in dread as he melts away into the greys of the water I am staring into.

"You wished to see the world," she speaks out of the water. "Behold, all you have said you desired! Welcome to the world of men and their many paradoxes. Solve them and save yourself."

I don't remember sitting down, but as I look around me, I realize I am on the ground in an ordinary field. There are no flowers anywhere about. The ground stretches around me, trees interrupting the space behind, the pond before me. I don't know where I am; I don't know where to go. I only know my love is dead, and my heart is a stone inside me.

SHADOWS

I wake up where I fell asleep, at first recalling the vivid field of flowers, but they begin to slip away from me . . . like my happiness.

What will happen to me? Will I be a sunflower picked, plucked, my petals thrown about? Will my bright yellow life now mingle with dirt and dew till nothing of me remains—until I become part of this earth? Is there nothing of me to withstand this reality she has placed me in?

I stand up, knowing that I have to walk. She wants me immobile, indecisive. I need to leave this field of nothing and find someone, go someplace. I must find my way in the world of men.

I hear someone crying, so I stop still and then proceed with caution. The sound stops as I near a hollowed-out tree. It's so strange—I'm outside now, but I still feel trapped. I don't know what to do and, for a moment, I do nothing. *This is what she wants*, I think, so I choose to move on.

"Is someone there?" My voice comes out sounding strange. "Can I be of service?"

There is a shuffle of movement and a creature comes out of the tree. She appears to be clothed in a collage of various furs. Her hair is dirty, but it seems yellow. Her tears have left streaks through the dirt on her face, and as I notice all this, I wonder what I myself must look like.

"Are you all right?" I try to smile, but I don't think it is successful by the way it feels on my face. I let it go and look down. I repeat what I've said in Latin, as she does not seem to understand me.

"Are you?" she falters. She speaks in a different tongue, but one that I am familiar with, so I nod.

That is all we say for a time. I don't know why she is here, what has brought her here—but somehow, just seeing her makes me feel I am not alone. I nod once and begin to turn around.

"Where are you going?" she asks.

"I'm going back to the pond. I must look a fright."

"Yes, well, I'm sure I could use a good washing myself. Would you mind showing me where it is?"

I nod again, wondering why I want to find out what her trouble has been.

We find it with ease and tidy up as best we can. I've not been able to say anything to her in all this time, though I want to. I want to ask her where she comes from, what happened to her, what she is doing here. I want to know—

My thoughts are interrupted with the sound of a horse a ways off. I turn to the girl, who is static, frozen with a horrified expression.

"What's wrong?"

"He mustn't find me!"

"What? Who—?"

"Please, help me hide; he must never find me." She does a strange thing. Out of a pocket in her furs, she pulls out a walnut and opens it, staining her face as dark as she can. She pulls over her hair a burlap hood, ties it under her chin, and then finishes by staining her hands.

The sounds of the horse fade away, and I stare at her in astonishment.

"Are you quite well?"

"Are you?" She looks through her brown eyes at me, and I wonder if she is mocking me.

I turn away again, but she stops me with a hand on my shoulder.

"I'm sorry, forgive me. I have no right to speak so harshly."

"Who are you hiding from?"

She looks away, "My father."

"I am sorry."

"Indeed, I wish I could have stayed forever."

"Where?"

"In his kingdom, in my home. But I have to find a new one."

I will not ask her more; she has spoken a great deal already. "Are you hungry?"

A smile tilts the right side of her darkened lips. "Famished."

"Well, I think we must learn how to forage." She nods and we set off back to the trees.

There are many things that one can find to eat in the forest; some are good, and some are bad. I hope she

knows which are which. There are berries and mushrooms, nuts and grubs. We are not desperate enough for
grubs, and the season for berries is gone, so we sample
everything else.

"What are you running from?"

A princess in distress seems to wonder things as well. I
stare at her and chew on a walnut. Without my flint I
cannot light a fire, which would be useful as the night soon
reminds us that autumn is coming soon. I will have to learn
without the witch's help. Perhaps this girl can teach me
how to hunt and we will survive quite well. Or maybe her
coat was a gift from her estranged father.

"Well, why are you here?"

I don't mean to, but out of instinct my hand reaches to
my frazzled head. "From the only mother I've known. I
had to leave."

She nods once. This is enough. There is no reason for
us to discuss any more, since it is a past neither of us will
be returning to. There is comfort in knowing that, if I must
be exiled, I have someone to be exiled with.

⌘

MY STOMACH CRAMPS began before dawn; hers must have
begun near the same time. Soon we were both sick and
exhausted. I tried to think of the exact mushrooms which
might have been toadstools, but I could not concentrate
long. By midday I passed out from exhaustion near her,
cursing my ignorance.

I suppose the hunters found us like that—passed out,
sick and filthy near the pond. It's amazing the horses did

not trample us. Having detected some life left in us, they gathered us with their game and returned to their fortress.

Time seemed a shifting thing. I could not tell night from day. Faces came in and out of my blurry vision. Our rescuers decided we would work as scullery maids to repay the lord for our care. But as our illness lingered, the head cook began to worry he would never get much use out of us. However, the cook's wife, Katherina, had more patience—and a great deal more knowledge of healing herbs and the benefits of rest.

After a week's illness, I began coming round, distinguishing light from shadow, reemerging from fits of dreams. Roughskin, for so they called the princess, had a harder time of it. When I was well enough, I began working in the kitchen and scullery. At night I returned to our sparse chambers, a tiny closet of a room tucked beneath a staircase next to the kitchen where Katherina had been caring for her. I would hold her hand and try to tell her she was safe.

"What do you know of her?" Katherina asked this evening.

"Only that she was done with the life she had lived, that was she was looking for a new one."

Katherina nods in silence, tucking a loose strand of white-blonde hair behind her right ear. Her face is round, with red apple cheeks, dark blue eyes around which flutter almost invisible white eyelashes. Her braided hair crowns her head, and with care she pulls her wimple and headdress over it before leaving. It makes me wonder that a kind and simple woman could marry a boar such as Jacobus.

Dark and grouchy, the smelly man daily shouts at us

underlings scrambling about the kitchen. As he works, he spouts what he feels is the best of all worldly knowledge, tormenting any who has ears they cannot close. There is one maid, Ursula, who is deaf and dumb; she seems to know what is needed and never has to listen to Jacobus. I find myself watching her with envy as her errands take her in and out of the kitchen. All day long he gives orders and snaps threats and insults, his face coarse, often sweating and red, making his white hair stand out from him like a mismatched stocking because he won't keep his head covered as decent people do. As the head baker and cook, he feels the need to order around the pantier, the bakers, the waferers, sauciers—so many of us!—and, of course, the kitchen and scullery maids. In an instant I am tired of him, and I begin to calculate out how long I will have to work before both Roughskin and I will have paid our debt and be free to leave. Of course, each day she is ill adds what I have subtracted the day before so that I fear we will never be free. She has been ill for two weeks now.

As I look at her, I wonder again about her masking her skin color, covering her beautiful hair with that hideous rag. I thought I would not question her past, for I do not want anyone to question my own—but I want to know. Poor Roughskin; her fate may be worse than mine if she does not rally.

"She must decide she wants to live." Katherina spoke in her hushed tone before she closed our door this evening.

I know she is right.

I sigh each day that I enter the massive kitchen to light candles before dawn. I then go outside to the enormous stone oven which is built into the southern wall. The days are a bustle of bone-breaking work, beginning with shoveling out soot and then sweeping out the entire oven. I am then back in the kitchen, readying and cleaning anything that was too hot to clean the night before. I set out everything on the work tables that the Boar will need for the midday meal and begin drawing water for the day. By this point, he has joined me in the kitchen and I assist him by running whatever errand he has in mind, or by doing whatever it is he feels is beneath him to do.

I am used to cleaning and cooking for one or two, not for hundreds, and so I am trying to adjust. This fortified dwelling houses not mere household servants, but an armory and barracks that are loyal to the lord and lady whose bread I now eat. The rest of the day is filled with cleaning before and after meals, scrubbing until I can no longer feel my hands. I try not to long for solitude, but it is a strange change to be always surrounded by others, hurried and bumped and continuously hearing and smelling them. By the end of the day I am quite worn, muscles aching, pungent from all my sweat and soot. I'm afraid I smell like Jacobus.

However difficult the day is, though, the nights are worse. I sit beside my friend in our tiny chamber where we share a straw mattress on the floor. I try to smile and to think of pleasant things as I bathe her face and arms with cool water from our one luxury, a clay basin. But after an hour or so, it seems pointless and I ready myself for bed, to begin the task of sleeping. All night long I am asleep but running, fleeing thoughts of my love, those dreams we had shared. What if Paul and I had escaped to this place? What life would we have led? Could I be keeping cottage for him? Would he have joined the lord's hunters?

Now that he is gone, it seems I learned too little of the details of his other life; I knew him without knowing him. I learned of his love for the wood, for scouting game, for speaking of kingdoms, for discussing land and its produce —but what of the details of his daily life? I am haunted by the things I did not learn. My dreams are incomplete and I rise to begin another day soured by the night.

Each morning is full of the same scouring of dishes, the same sweeping of ashes, lighting of fires, filth through and through. By the time I return to our chamber to relieve Katherina in the evening, I am dirtier than ever before in my life. If Roughskin would revive and work beside me, she would not need to darken her skin again.

⌒⟨≈⟩⌒

AT LENGTH, three weeks after our arrival, Katherina bursts into the kitchen, blessing me by interrupting one of her husband's unrelenting tirades. "Her fever has broken! She is on the mend. You will have your friend back soon."

I think I must be crying, but I'm not sure why. There is no sound coming from me, but my eyes are wet and the others are staring. "Excuse me," I say as I hurry away.

I hear the Boar begin to protest, but his wife shushes him with sweet words, reminding him that now she will be able to be at home more. I'd not thought of that; I will miss her.

I don't know what's wrong with me, but I finish crying in the large pantry, as Peter, our pantier, is away gathering stores to get us through the week. I breathe in the smell of cedar mingled with grains and root vegetables. I find I rather enjoy the darkness since I didn't bring a light with me when I exited. I feel safer here than anywhere I have been in a long time. I take a deep breath and dry my eyes with the corner of my apron. I spend the rest of the day working hard, looking forward to the evening when I can visit with Roughskin.

"Are you feeling better?" I ask on entering our chamber as I see her eyelids are open.

She smiles at my return. "Are you?"

"I think so."

"Well, you look a fright." She laughs a bit but cuts off with a few coughs. She sits up with great effort.

I take off my raggedy wimple and walk over to the basin kind Katherina must have replenished with water before leaving. "Then I should be grateful that there are no mirrors to see myself in."

"Indeed."

"Did Katherina already leave?" It is obvious she must have.

"She seemed very tired and I told her to go. She's been very good to us, hasn't she?"

I smile at the girl. "Yes."

"It will be difficult to repay her."

"No, she is not one to ask for repayment—but her husband does." I display the calluses I am developing from my labors.

"I see." Her brown eyebrows lift. They are patchy as they are growing in; it is obvious the princess once plucked them and her hairline to achieve that fashionable high forehead that seems so popular among the ladies I have glimpsed here. "Well, I once said I wanted to be useful in this world. I guess we will see if I really meant it."

I finish cleaning up as best I can.

"In your other life" —she whispers, as though she is treading on a wound—"did you no work?"

"I did, but it was mostly for myself."

She nods again.

"Do you still need to hide your skin?" I ask, matching her quiet tone.

Her brow furrows. "Perhaps I should, though maybe they are no longer looking . . ." Her voice drifts away as she ponders the stub of our tallow candle. "Do you always work this late?"

"The scullery maid is the first up starting fires, and the

last to bed after cleaning the kitchen. It's an important and laborious job."

She smiles at my description. "Are there no others?"

"Of course there are—we are merely the kitchen maids, but there is a full staff, crowded with countless servants, many who work in and around the kitchen, while others never see the kitchen. I think we'll manage."

"Well, then, you will have to teach it all to me tomorrow."

"No, lie in bed at least one more day; you will be no use to me tomorrow."

The silence is awkward at first, our conversation laced with things we cannot speak about, threaded with things we fear. Perhaps one day I will tell her of my other life. For now, it is enough to know she is going to be well.

⌘

THE DAYS FALL INTO ROUTINE. Now that Roughskin is well, she works in the kitchen, and at certain things she is useful. She is unused to cleaning as hard as we must, so I find myself finishing what she does not. However, she makes wonderful soup which she serves me a few times a week when we have been left very late to clean up whatever Jacobus deems is our duty. We treat ourselves to solitude and soup, and I find finishing those dishes the easiest of all my work.

"My mother taught me how," she smiles, a fond memory distracting her.

"I did not know that queens cooked."

She looks startled that I have guessed her nobility. "But how—"

I laugh at her shocked face and smooth my hair-rag with the back of my hand. "That first day, you said you wished that you could return to your father's kingdom. A princess alone would own a kingdom as her father's."

She shakes her head at her own folly. "And I thought I was so clever . . ."

"I am the only one who knows, and I will keep your secret as you have kept mine."

"But I don't know yours."

"You know I cannot return to my old life; you know enough."

"We have, both of us, begun anew."

"Indeed," I nod, and take another swallow of the soup, glad that our day is over and everyone else has bedded down. "Now about your mother and her soup . . ."

Roughskin quirks her patchy eyebrow up as she reminisces. "My mother was of noble blood, and the women in her family passed down a great many traditions, including certain recipes of soup. The one soup I have not made you was a fairy recipe given to my—" She pauses to count back "—great-great-great grandmother. By it, she wed a prince."

"I see."

"Of course you don't." Her brown eyes twinkle as she begins the tale in earnest. "You see, a long time ago, fairies had a great regard for the common people; they found that many of them were more royal than those of noble lineage."

"Oh!" I love to see her enthralled in the story, her nut-brown face lifted in happiness.

"Yes, and above all, my many greats-grandmother's family was ordinary, common. They lived in the land and cared for their neighbors, and the fairies found them a worthy clan. When the fairy queen's daughter became ill, it was to my family that they flew her, and with dew from an enchanted rose, she grew well. As payment—though, of course, my family insisted in vain they should not be paid—the fairies passed along a recipe for good health. What they did not tell them was that it promoted love as well. So when a wandering prince came by, quite famished from the hunt, my innocent great-great-great grandmother made him the soup—"

"—And your family became a noble family!" I clap my hands together.

She shakes her head as though at a recalcitrant pupil. "Come now, weren't you listening, Rapunzel? They were already noble, but at last they became known as noble."

I nod at her mocking of me. "I understand your meaning. For whom have you made the soup?"

She quiets and looks away.

A STORY

There is a troubadour who has come with a band of players to entertain the lord and his court. It is exhilarating; I have never seen any of their kind before. It seems that the Church looks down on rebel troupes of this sort, as all players *should* be working alongside the Church or in the care of a royal house. These renegades, however, have caught the admiration of our lord, who attends the morning mass in order catch a nap before beginning his day, and always breaks fast in the mornings instead of piously waiting till midday to avoid the sin of gluttony, as many noblemen do.

This troupe's tunics are split down the middle with the right side in blue and the left side in yellow, unlike our lord whose colors are red and green. The leggings match their tunics. Some uncouth players remove their head coverings when they enter the heat of the kitchen to grab food and ale after entertaining the nobles. I have overheard from the maids who serve in the court that the players have filled the Great Hall with raucous laughter and awe every night this past week. I feel myself aching to partake in the fun. But I know that I am a mere kitchen maid, an ugly baldish one at that, and so I keep these feelings to myself for now.

I know Roughskin struggles even more than I. What must her life have been like in her father's kingdom? She is unused to serving and to being shut out. From time to time I have heard her crying into her bedding at night, and I try to lie still so that she won't be embarrassed for my hearing her.

The Boar has been harping all day about the pains he has endured from the extra work from the harvest festivities. I am tired of hearing it, but now he says he is so put out he can no longer work and we will have to finish for him. It is fortunate there is not a great deal left on the feast, but the dishes pile up without mercy, and it is into the morning before we can get to bed. If I did not think it would wound Katherina, I might try to find a way to rid us of the Boar forever—but perhaps these are just the violent thoughts of a fatigued servant.

⋯

TONIGHT THE ENTERTAINERS have come to see us again in the kitchen. They have opted to entertain us while they eat, entering with loud jests. One of the jugglers marches over to Roughskin while she scrubs and tries to get her to try her hand at his craft. She laughs, amused, and asks him to juggle the dishes; he amazes us by doing so without dropping a single one. Good thing, too, as I don't know what the Boar would do had one broken. I am overwhelmed with the players' presence. They seem a coarse sort, but when their sole attention is not focused on me, I am able to enjoy their antics.

The troubadour has promised a tale while we clean, but he refuses to take requests. Once the troupe has sat around the large rectangular work table, he pulls out a strange instrument he calls a lute. It is flat on one side and round on the back, fat at one end and narrows into a neck. He holds the neck with one hand away from his body and holds the fat end in front of his belly. He then uses his fingers to strum and hold down strings that run the length of the hollow instrument, creating a beautiful sound. Into the wood, there is embedded a beautiful pink flower, which I take to be the mark of his trade. His voice is a mixture of sadness and joy, traveling with the music and the story:

Nearby, he sings, a queen whose beauty is untarnished begins to die. Taking her husband's hands in her own, she makes a dying wish, that her husband promise to remarry one whose beauty equals her own. The king grieves his queen for years and looks alone to his daughter for comfort. But one day, on the advice of his counselors, he at long last sets out to find a queen. One is not fair enough, another too lean; each has a defect that makes them of less value than the late queen. Again the king returns to his hearth and finds comfort in his wife's lone legacy, his daughter. He begins noticing how fair she has grown, how lovely, how like his wife. He realizes her beauty might one day even surpass that of his late queen . . .

The troubadour's notes grow wary, full of ominous undertones as he tells of the daughter's fear at her father's intentions and her insistence that he complete three impossible tasks before she would consent to marry him. As the king completed each task, the girl began to plan. The notes begin to run as he tells of the girl's flight, but the thrumming sounds stop as he flattens the strings with his hand.

"And then?" one of the players prods.

"I've yet to write the ending." The troubadour smiles, bows to us and heads out of the kitchen.

"Best not to present it until you have!" the player calls after, and the rest sit around jesting, making our work grow longer as now they need more drink.

⊂⊇⊇⊃⊃

I'M EXHAUSTED THIS MORNING. Each time I feel that I am close to finishing dishes, more get brought in, or the cook begins another tirade about something being dirty, or something in this vein. Roughskin is no help. Ever since last night she has been distant and moody. The festivities will continue tonight, which means more work, and I'm tired enough to faint.

The Boar is barking at Roughskin now. "Well, if you can't be any use here, run to the market and raise up more help for this evening, for it is certain we won't make it by with you moping about."

His insufferable griping is just too much, and I feel as though I'm going to do something rash. I feel a great desire to thrash him, to smack the back of his head with his favorite pot, but I take a deep breath. I remind myself there is no need for violence so I refrain, knowing that it would serve no purpose. Besides, it would leave Roughskin and I to finish preparing for the remaining three-day feast without any help.

It is a long and hot afternoon, the kitchen boiling with smells that I can no longer distinguish. I feel sick and hungry at the same time. Three girls have wandered in and been set to work, which will help the maid staff. Roughskin returns and beckons me to her.

"I don't mean to abandon you, but I will return as soon as I can."

"Where are you going?"

"If anyone asks, I am unwell."

It is true she is unwell; her eyes are feverish and her skin would be hot to touch, but I know that her illness has not returned. I know where she is going. "I understand. We must all find our place."

She looks as though she longs to say something, but she closes her mouth and agrees to help me as long as possible.

UNMASKED

Right before the evening meal, I watch as she slips off, and another girl ambles in from the market to help me with the feast's dishes. We run in and out to keep the fires going for the Boar.

He does not notice Roughskin's departure until far into the evening when the girl and I are struggling to finish the mounds of dishes.

"And where has your friend gone?" he sneers.

"She said to say she was unwell. She stayed as long as she could, but I knew she needed to go—"

"So you felt free to give her leave?"

He is tired and irrational at this point, so I keep my peace.

"The lord's son will likely call for a bowl of soup after the ball—he always does. My wife has told me Roughskin makes a good soup. Let her make it and take it to him. If I hear that even a hair falls into it—"

"Roughskin will take it to his man herself and he can

berate her if he should find it. No blame will be cast on you." I sound calm, though my thoughts are not.

The Boar nods once. "Tomorrow will be another long day. Make sure it is spotless before you bed!" With this last growl, he exits.

I look around the kitchen, dismayed with the stacks of dishes on the counters and worktable—but though I will ache tomorrow, tonight I will see it done.

I hear the music lilting down the stone corridors as the kitchen doors swing open and shut with the coming and going of servants. I pause in my work to imagine Roughskin in all her glory. I know not how she will manage, but she will hold the interest of the court and appear once more as a princess, her beauty surpassing that of her mother's.

"If the girl is unwell, how will she manage to make—"

"She'll be fine," I interrupt my helper. The docile girl nods and we continue our chores.

Before long, I excuse myself to get Roughskin, hoping she has returned. As I open the door, there is a glimmer of sunlight, and I shut the door in haste so that no one else will see Roughskin, the fair princess.

"Is the dancing over?"

She seems to be shining, seeing something I cannot see. I wish I could take back my words, because as soon as they are said, the light leaves her face. "It is, for me." She takes off her dress of sunlight and folds it to fit inside her walnut, then begins to disguise herself once more with the soot and ashes that are so common to our trade. I tell her of the cook's command. Soon the kitchen is filled with the savory aromas of simmering soup and I beg a spoonful.

Roughskin complies and my mouth fills with an herbed broth thickened with cream and potatoes. I want more, but there is no time if we are ever to rest, so I return to work as Roughskin takes her offering away. After finishing our tasks, we fall into a great heap of sleeping bones. With my last thought, I doubt if we will have the strength to get up and do it all again on the morrow.

⚬✦⚬

WE DO. I hate it, but we do. The day is even busier than the last and the Boar even crosser, for as soon as we step into the kitchen he grabs Roughskin by the ear and begins cursing her. "What did you put into that soup, little tart? The lord's son is very angry and knows I did not make it; you are to go and see him at once. Do your best to mend, or you'll not get a morsel from me again, you wretch!"

As soon as her back has disappeared, I question the cook.

"He found something in his soup that made him unhappy—now get back to work!"

It was not only that, I found out later. The princess had placed a golden ring in the bowl and the prince knew, even before he found it, that it was too good to be the cook's soup. The handmaid of the lady, who never mixes with our sort, sent a lower maid to investigate the girl of rough-skins, and—like all maids—she seems to tell more than she learns.

At the ball, an incognito princess had appeared, and the lord-to-be had fallen in love with her. He held on as long as he could, but she slipped away before the ball had ended. In a distraught temper he went to have his regular soup, as his stomach was often upset after feasting. He could seldom sleep after such revelry, and now there, in his bowl, was a golden ring. Of course, the cook knew nothing about it and Roughskin cried innocent as well. The young man was fooled, but the lady knew something to be amiss and thus the lower maid was to follow us around all day, to see if the young kitchen maids were thieving or playing tricks on her son.

What joy is mine to work with a boar, a gloomy princess, and a suspicious maid! At least my thoughts are occupied and I will be too tired to think tonight.

Again, the young girl from the market appears when Roughskin excuses herself. Fortunate for me, the suspicious maid has been called away by many tasks at this point. I take a calming breath and content myself with thoughts of suds and hot water, keeping fires burning, and clearing soot and ashes when all but one stove is cooled.

The cook gives himself another early night, demanding that Roughskin send the lord's son and himself a bowl of soup. In his mind, the Boar is a king of the kitchen, so why should his minions not serve him? Perhaps he hopes to claim a golden ring as well.

❧

TODAY IS as strange as the last few days, with rumors of the sunlight maiden now coupled with that of the silvery moon maiden who appeared last night. I caught a glimpse of the dress before Roughskin tucked it away. I was right: she looked glorious. It is no wonder the lord's son suffered indigestion when he lost sight of her.

He now claims to have found a golden spinning wheel in Roughskin's soup, though no one can explain to me the size. It all seems peculiar and ludicrous at once, making me doubt the sanity of the lord-to-be. But her ladyship's maid assures me it is all true—after all, the lady told the handmaid who told her . . . And then, Roughskin was summoned again.

⊰⊱

She seems more distant than ever, more confused and bewildered, but also elated, as though somehow she has found something—something she is unsure of but excited by. I do not know how to aid or support her. The game she is playing is quite dangerous, to rouse the interest of the heir to a lord while playing the humble role of a maid. It is absurd. Perhaps it is in her blood, and the fairies cursed her great-great-great-grandmother with daftness. Or perhaps I have just not been prepared to understand the eccentricities of the world of men. Or—perhaps they're all just mad.

"What are you doing?" I ask her when, for a moment, we are alone.

"What do you mean?" She plays dumb. It is quite unbecoming.

"You are asking to be put down. They are noble; they can kill you with a tap of their fingers."

I have never seen her rise to her full stature; she is taller than I thought. "I am royal, and they will soon recognize me as their equal."

"Then why not just tell them?"

"Because *I* would not believe me." Her smile is tender. Perhaps she thinks of me as a nice pet. "Rapunzel, I do not belong in this world, but unless I am married to a lord I will not be safe in theirs. Don't you understand? This is the one way that I know to untangle my life. Nobility loves nothing as much as a riddle or mystery. I am that riddle. They alone must solve it, or they will resent me. This is how the game is played."

I think I must be staring, because she stops here.

"Have you had no contact with nobility?"

Had she thought I had? "I have had no contact with anyone." I return to the drudgery of the day, knowing that by nightfall I will have lost her.

⚬⚬⚬

BY MORNING ALL IS KNOWN. The sunlight maiden, the maiden of the moonlight dress, the incognito maiden of the dress of stars who appeared at the last three nights of the feast is, in fact, the daughter of a king. Her father was determined to marry her and so she commanded that he do the impossible. She told him he must have the sun sewn into one gown, the moon and then the stars into two others, before she would consent to wed him. He had it accomplished, and so she set before him another task, one she hoped more impossible than the others. She asked for a coat fashioned with the hide of each of the animals of the forest. So great was his lust that he cared not that killing so many animals would leave his people hungry and he had it made. With the coat, she masked herself and escaped into the wood, helped first by fairy magic and then by hunters from a nearby kingdom where she became a maid. Of course, after dancing and enchanting the lord's son with her beauty, her soup, and the final token, the golden hook, she allowed him to reveal who she was. Now they are to be wed with the blessing of his parents and the Church.

The kitchen is buzzing with plans for the upcoming wedding, and the young market girl takes her permanent place at my side as the new maid. The Boar feels himself quite important and Katherina asks me if I knew all along of the princess's true identity.

I did, of course—but I do not tell her that. I simply go out for a walk that evening and never return.

WITHIN THE WOOD

Tonight I hear the rising pitch of the wind as though it is gathering for a storm—but instead of a storm, my witch speaks, her raggedy voice carried by the wind.

"How fare you, my child?"

"Well enough." I am proud of the snapping fire I have started, aided by new knowledge learned as a kitchen maid. The evening air is chilled, and I pull my blankets close about me in the darkness of the wood where I have decided to rest, my small pack nearby, ready to act as my lumpy pillow.

"You were never cold atop my tower." Her face glows out of the orange and gold of the blaze.

"I was never warm atop your tower," I counter. "You never let me know what warmth meant."

"But you were content there. Now you are cold and abandoned."

"I am not cold and I am not abandoned. There was nothing for me in the last kingdom, so I have journeyed on.

I am seeking—" I stop. I do not know what it is that I am seeking. Why did I leave? I don't know, I felt confused and confined and as though I had to get away before I was smothered. Once Roughskin had found her place, I knew I needed to go find my own.

"You have your freedom, what more could you want?"

"I want my love back," I choke.

"At least you've been loved!" her voice rages. "You were safe and well in my care, but you dismissed it. What have you risen to? The poverty-stricken peasant? The kitchen maid?" She mocks me.

"I am making my way in the world. That is what you wanted, isn't it? For me to see how horrible it is? How difficult?"

"You think I'm right?" she grasps.

"No, I know you to be wrong. The world of men is full of hardship, but it is full of life—and I prefer a cold death to being imprisoned in your tower!" I whip back.

"Very well, enjoy your solitude. Enjoy your lengthening list of people you miss. Enjoy the sound of wolves sniffing your feet as you slumber." And she is gone once more, but I do not care. I am not finished yet.

⚬⚬

THIS WOOD IS DENSE, full of thorns and roots that trip. Perhaps I should stay by the roadside, but something primal shudders; I feel as a woman traveling alone I must not. I journey parallel to it and watch for signs of life. My eyes look around for dwellings, for market towns; my ears listen for sounds of wildlife. I have brought bread and cheese with me as well as a small bladder in which I collect water from a brook that I follow through this wood.

It is not silent among these trees. There is the sound of insects humming and birds singing, but it feels hushed compared to the bustle of the kitchen. I am stronger than when I lived alone in my tower, and I can travel much farther than I ever imagined due to my labor in the kitchen. I am stretching the bread and cheese as best I can, wary of mushrooms. I am fortunate to find juicy apples, tart pears, and the last of the tangy apricots among some of the trees.

I'm often amazed that fruit, a by-product of a tree's life, can extend to preserve my own. Who designed this wonderful gift of life? Who orchestrates this strange melody?

As painful as the silence has been at times, I find myself having these thoughts, and I speculate as to whether it will heal my soul to question the making of the universe. The world is knit with care, with precision, and yet it has a seed of restlessness in it, one that leads to lust and anger, to betrayal and irrational cravings. Why was it made this way, this beautiful world of men, with this deep flaw?

This is like the other questions I tried to reason out with my beloved in our evenings. I can see Paul's smile now, how he would stare at me in amazement, how he would chuckle and then clear his throat. "Most women don't question such things," he once told me when I had voiced one such question. "Some might think it blasphemous, a sin against God."

"What do you think?" I asked him.

"I think God gave you a mind with which to reason, a

mind with which to think. He is not afraid of your questions."

"No?"

"No."

I loved the way he would look at me, with a sense of awe and distraction at my intellect, and sometimes amusement. I often questioned, if we did leave the tower and traveled out into the rest of the world, would I still hold his fascination? Would he tire of me and my questions someday?

I suppose it's best not to know.

◌◌

MY FEET HOLD a rhythm in their walk, rustling through the fresh-fallen leaves beneath them. My body grows stronger with each step, and my mind expands to understand the world that has opened up before me. I did not anticipate how my feet and legs would hurt in the evenings, though I suppose I will get used to it as I did when I worked for the Boar on the cold stone floor of the kitchen and scullery.

Ah! To be outside! The sky that peeks through seems a brilliant blue this morning, crowded by trees who adorn themselves in the brightest hues of autumn. There is a smell in the wind reminiscent of smoke that I've always longed to be surrounded by. I used to catch a hint of it when the season would grow chilly. I remember wanting to jump out and touch it when I was smaller, and my witch, seeing my joy in autumn, gathered up the leaves and we jumped in the pile to play woodland elfin games.

I remember my childhood; we were happiest then, before the days when books were my one comfort.

It's funny—I have not read a book since leaving my tower. They were all that I loved for the longest time. Even when I became dissatisfied with their vicarious truths I still returned to them—but now, I don't miss them. They taught me all they could and now I must learn for myself. Is that what this journey is to teach me? Is that what I am to learn?

⸎

IT IS surprising that I have not come across a single house or barn in this whole week of traveling. One would think that I would have at least seen a few in the wood, but somehow I have seen no man, woman, or child in all this time. And now that my cheese is gone and the bread is a morsel, I know that it is time for me to set out to find something, to find someone I must return to the road, perhaps . . . But just as I decide this, I notice a space behind several trees that seems brighter up ahead. I move toward it and discover a clearing in the middle of the wood, what looks like a field harvested not long ago. Beyond it, I spot a cottage and another building of some sort nearby. I will go to see if they have any work in exchange for a nice meal and a place to stay the night. I do not know if that is appropriate, but I will only find the answer if I try.

The lady of the house is a large, fair-haired woman and quite cordial as she asks me what my business is. I tell her that I am traveling and ask if she has any work for a meal and night's rest.

"Just one meal?" She smiles down at me.

"Well," I feel unsure, "I suppose that would depend on the amount of work."

"Indeed it would," her nod invites me inside. "How long have you been traveling?" She asks as she leads me through the spacious home.

"A week," I say, looking around me. This is not the mud and wattle home of a peasant with one room, but neither is it the home of nobility. Perhaps a merchant, but why so far from the road? I wonder as she leads me to the back room of the grey wood dwelling. The long room is the kitchen and there is a large rectangular work table that doubles for dining. There are two chairs on either end and two benches on the long sides tucked under, out of the way. Near the back wall, there is a chimney with soot marks shooting up above its mouth with a stove on which to cook. It is cluttered with pans and pots and has a fireplace beneath that acts as an oven. Next to this, hiding in a corner is a small alcove—cozy in the evenings, I'm sure. In the opposite corner is tinder and chopped wood to keep the fires going, but I imagine the rest of the wood outside the door I see.

The mistress is looking at me in eager anticipation. "And where are you going?"

"I am not sure."

"Do you think you might stay on awhile?" She looks around the room but returns her expectant gaze at me.

"I don't know. Do you have need of a servant?"

"I have need of a good servant for a short time. I have a great many relatives coming this way, and though I have hired Cook"—she gestures to the stout woman who has just hurried in from outdoors—"I do need someone else to help with a maid's work."

"I see."

"I was going to head to the market town just west of here, but if you are willing and get along with Cook, you will have saved me a trip."

I look at Cook who offers a silent, shy nod. "How long do you need help?"

"A fortnight or so. No more than a month's time."

Her mannerisms in no way remind me of one used to commanding servants. Though she is not pleading with me to stay, she is kind and acts as though my staying would be a favor. This is not at all like I was treated in the Boar's kitchen.

"I would be happy to stay if my service pleases you."

Again her smile is broad and she shows me the duties that will be required of me. The quiet Cook comes forward and we are introduced. She is known as Helga, and I know she will be more pleasant to work with than Jacobus.

⤝⤞

LIFE in the cottage is busy but quiet. It is full of an odd peace, though I try to remind myself that it may not stay that way once the relatives arrive. I find Helga whirling about, preparing various pleasantries for her guests.

All of the rooms are cleaned and aired, though it seems they were not dirty, just unused. I change the bedding with new straw, and the whole house begins to smell sweet and fresh. The floors are whitewashed, though the walls don't need such attention. Each night, I sleep in the small alcove in the kitchen. I was right—it is cozy to sleep indoors near the hearth. Cook takes the room attached to the kitchen that I mistakenly assumed led outdoors.

Two days before the company arrives, all other chores are done and I help Cook organize the kitchen. She has just come back from the market town nearby to gather all that she did not have in the cellar. Most of the vegetables and herbs are easily stored, and the meats are to be brought by the master himself later today when he said he should return from hunting.

I am happy with my fare, but somehow, there seems a lack somewhere. I should be content—but again, something is missing.

THEY ARRIVE in great loads and I wonder where we will put them all. This is not a castle, after all, but a cottage. It seems, though, they all fit in the eight bedrooms. All of the men bear a striking resemblance with their grey eyes, square jaws, and broad foreheads. They are also tan from their time outdoors, readying their homes for the coming winter. They are not a grand lot, but a simple group of relatives, coming together to decide something of great import—I know not what.

Cook is busy. I help her as best I can, but then I must clean myself up, donning a fresh surcoat and wimple to hide my scraggly hair. I want to be presentable while I serve the relatives. My mistress provided this fresh change of clothes and I am grateful to have something to wear when I do my wash each week.

The evening meal is served with little concern, though the men drink a great deal more than I thought they would. The women seem quiet and worry over their food, as though they are waiting to be dismissed.

After the cooked pears are served, the master nods to his wife who leads the women in leaving the room. The men stand until they are gone and then disappear—to drink, perhaps to discuss what is to be decided. I clear the trenchers and begin the great process of cleaning, missing having a helper. Still, I prefer to work here with soft-spoken Cook who allows me to think and work without too much interference. I think this is mutually appreciated.

She finishes her work and heads to bed, tired from her labor at the stove and oven. I continue to heat water and wash dishes, stopping to check with increasing frequency and see if anything else needs to be done, making certain each room has water in its pitcher for bedtime.

❧

THE DAYS SEEM to melt into one another and I long to be out of this house, though I do not know why. My job here is much better than my last, and though I work hard, I know I am getting paid and that I am appreciated—as much as any maid might be. Helga is well-pleased with me and I should be at ease, but I am not. Something does not sit well.

Perhaps I miss the princess too much. At night I knew we would talk, and though we were guarded in what we said, we could at least discuss the day's events. Now most times I go an entire day and never have a full conversation. I do not know why this is bothersome, but it is.

❧❧❧

THE DECISION BEING MADE, it hangs over them like an ominous cloud, threatening to rain—but the pressure mounts and is never released. It seems an eternity since the guests arrived, and each night the men discuss the question in privacy, hushing each time I check on them. The faces of the women grow tight and their plates remain full; Cook is wary of preparing food for them, uncertain how much they will eat.

Something is not right here; I can feel it, but I can scarce name it. It is in my mistress's smile, which once filled her face but now barely finds a corner in which to hover. My master's deep voice becomes gruff as the days travel along, and each of the men follows suit. There is no longer any revelry in their taking of meals, and the women do not act like women. They speak little, if at all.

I have wondered all along where their children are, for there are none about, and none are spoken of. Something is not right here, but no one will name it.

THE SECRET

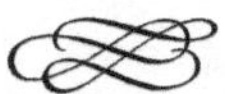

I have learned their secret at last, though I dread to think of it. They are one and all barren. A curse was placed on their heads—in truth, on their mother's head, as the brothers are all sons of the same mother. None of the women can birth a babe due to the curse. It seems that a witch was greatly offended (aren't they always?) by their mother, and she was cursed to have sterile sons. Each son married and thought to carry on the family name, but not a child has been born. They gathered this year to decide what to do since their dying mother had at last revealed the nature of the curse, but their talks seem as fruitless as they. For who can fight a witch?

THE COOK LEFT us this morning, vowing she will not stay in a house so cursed. She crossed her chest as a sign when she left and spit to the side as though to get rid of the taste. I cannot leave. Though I am not bound to these people, I know more than I hope they ever will of witches and curses. Indeed, I know there must be some way of helping them. When Helga came in this morning and saw me cooking, she knew what had happened with Cook. Her great happy face faltered, tears dripping down her rosy cheeks.

The sisters have all decided to take turns cooking, which is something they enjoy doing. I cannot remember their names, but their conversations are interesting, even if they do crowd the place somewhat. Some are standing around the dark-stained work table, one cutting up cheese while another is slicing up the coarse barley bread Cook made yesterday. My mistress is absorbed in cutting up fruit for cooking, and soon the women are relaxing while sweet and savory scents fill the air.

"I thought I would be able to birth a great many babies when I married so young," the one married to the eldest says as she fries up salted fish. She speaks loudly, as her back is turned to the women at the work table while she hunches over the stove.

"As did I," says another with raven hair as she peeks from behind at the fish. The kitchen now begins to smell salty, which seems to further soothe the women. Since they have tied their apron strings over their surcoats, they have loosed their tongues to discuss and unravel what their husbands cannot. "I came from a large family, as did he. I felt sure we would have many young sons by this point. We would be happy to farm and—"

"Curse their mother's appetite! Did she have to be so greedy?" the youngest bride cries out. One would not think she who was so quiet-looking with her mousy brown hair and large blue eyes would be so vehement.

"Come now," Helga tries to appease, brushing a loose blonde lock behind her ear, "we have all been greedy from time to time."

"Yes, but her greed led her to sin against a witch!"

"And who would you have her sin against?" the raven one asks, the furrow between her eyebrows evidence of the years they have all spent questioning their fate.

I continue my chore, toting in water from the well in the yard, catching snippets of their exchange from time to time. They seem to feel better the more they talk, though it has been the opposite for their husbands.

"Our men long for action, but how can they fight an enemy they cannot see?" Helga mumbles. "Let us send them out to hunt—this will make them feel useful. Besides, we will need more food soon enough. While they are gone, I believe if we continue to think on it, we can solve this problem ourselves."

"You think us above our men?"

"I believe the witch a woman—and who but a group of women can see her follies and weaknesses?"

The women agree, and before midmorning the men gather supplies and leave, anxious to be accomplishing something.

"Yes, yes, go," one of the wives laughs. "It will do you good to kill something!"

They wave their husbands goodbye and fall to discussing the particulars of the curse, their hands busy as they knit and mend in the great room before a rosy fire after the midday meal. I serve them tea in chipped cups that have been well-used.

"Perhaps it is our belief that gives the curse its strength," the quiet mouse reasons.

"That cannot be it, because it was strong before we knew of it." The eldest wife speaks rocking while she knits methodically.

"Yes, but now we know, we believe."

"Because we have seen the proof." The raven one argues.

"Because we are afraid." The eldest resolves.

This brings silence, and the women continue their sewing and knitting in quiet for a time, my mistress rocking back and forth keeping the women working in rhythm.

"Aren't most curses broken by a sacrifice?" I start at this, almost spilling the tea. I look up, I want to look to see who has spoken. I cannot recognize her voice, but I have missed my chance to see who it was.

"That is true." I hear caution in the eldest's voice. "But you would have to find the witch to make a sacrifice."

"And what is it she would want?" my mistress asks at last.

"I believe most witches are lonely, so they require the first-born." The first voice speaks again.

"The first-born of all?" The young bride seems shocked.

"Perhaps not—what would she want with so many children? No, but she might require the first of us to give birth to also give up the child."

The silence is weighted.

"Wouldn't she have said so already?" The raven one sounds squeamish.

"To whom? The mother? No, she would not give their mother peace for her sin."

"I know I would not find peace in knowing that my grandchild was raised by a witch."

"So you are not willing to give up your first-born, eh, Regina?" Helga queries a honey-haired girl not much older than the youngest bride.

"Indeed, I am not. I would rather be barren."

"You are! We all are. As long as this curse remains intact, we will all be barren with no children to give our husbands, no families to love, no babes to cuddle. Why have we breasts, if not to suckle? Why have we arms, if not to hold? What use is this rocking chair if not for quieting and sending a small one off to slumber? Have you not dreamed of it? Each of us in our hearts, no matter the sacrifice, are we not determined to make it?"

I am startled by my mistress's poignant speech, I feel her pain as my own, and I wonder about my mother. Where is she? How much does she ache to know that a witch has raised her child? Was her punishment worth her greed?

These women are now willing to pay; each and every one is willing to send off their husband to make amends with a witch. The men will return and then be off again in search of her so that they might have a future.

THE MURDER

I cannot bear to stay. Helga thinks it the curse that I am fleeing. She pays me, wishes me well, and I leave, determined to put all thoughts of them and their sacrificed child well behind me as I go deeper into the wood.

A wood, or forest, is a wondrous thing. I used to stare out my tower at the trees I could see beyond the fortress wall, wondering what it would be like to be utterly surrounded by trees. Now I know one feels small next to the majesty and untouched beauty of the wood, stretching high above me, their branches laden with leaves turning all sorts of colors. The gold, oranges, and brilliant reds swirl to the ground, dancing through the air and crunching when they dry and grow brittle beneath my feet. I shiver a bit and wrap myself tightly in the shawl given me by my former mistress. The air is full of the scent of pine and leaf mold. I close my eyes for a moment and imagine curses do not exist, that this moment can be as beautiful as the trees around me seem to promise. I open my eyes and smile; the past is behind me, and I will make a new future for myself, somewhere in this lovely, precarious world.

⌘

I AWOKE HEARING IT: a man singing. He was journeying through the wood, though why he was walking so early in the morning, I do not know. The moon was bright through the thinned leaves; perhaps he was too excited to sleep. His song did sound joyful—but all at once his voice stopped. I think I was just beginning to rouse when an ugly, deep voice rang out, something about *not worthy*. It was a harsh tone, and I was grateful I had chosen a sheltered place in which to sleep so that I could not be seen. I heard a scuffle, and then I moved to see their forms in the distance, fighting. It finally occurred to me that if I could see them, they might be able to see me, so I was quick to move myself to cower by some bushes and a stump.

There was a gasp, then two thumps when a body hit the ground in separate pieces. I heard the survivor laughing and digging, burying the remains. My ears burned and I felt like howling in rage. It didn't matter that I didn't know the victim. I cannot fathom how one person can kill another and then laugh about it. He was whistling while he buried the remains, his breath hitting the cold air in hot puffs of smoke.

I did a strange thing then: I followed the murderer, for I was quite sure he had sought out the other man in the solitude of the wood to do away with him. I have never followed anyone before, and I will not say that I was subtle, simply determined in my task. I believe the man was too happy with his occupation to notice the scurrying behind him.

After a time, with the sun beginning to light the sky, we came to a small mud-and-wattle dwelling in a clearing. The hovel looks as though it has been woven together with twigs, branches, and moss. I noticed the man put away his shovel and clean himself before heading inside, only to rise and come back outside as though he had been asleep and now must begin the day's labor.

The windows were shut, all but the one at a young girl's bedroom, where a rose bush was in bloom despite the frost. She was rising and singing, and it reminded me of the bit of song I had heard from the murdered man.

"So your love is gone, is he?" The murderer spoke as he passed her room to return outside. "He has left you? I told you he was not worthy of you."

"He has not abandoned me. Once he has found a place for us, he will return for me."

"I am sure he will return for you," he scorned her. I watched as he made his way out of the house and headed, I suppose, towards town.

I sat still, wondering what course of action to take. It was obvious what had happened, but it was unclear what I should do for the girl. Was it better for her to wait and never hear from her love, or to know that he had been murdered—and worse, murdered by the man who seemed to be her brother and guardian? I recalled the night I waited so long for my beloved to come to me, the night he had been unable to come, and I made my decision. I will do what little I can.

NIGHT HAS COME. The brother has returned from town and, after drinking too much ale, has gone to bed. I have heard the girl singing with a quiet, sad voice all day long while she cleaned the house and cured her fruits in the kitchen. Tonight as she sings, I watch tears soften the contours of her shadowed face near her candle. She bows her head and kneels beside her bed, praying, I believe, for the safety of the murdered man. It is in vain, but she does not know yet.

I wait until her breathing has evened in sleep and then I travel to her window and sing back to her. She awakens and believes it is a dream. She seems to mistake me for an angel or elf and follows without a word to the grave. There she finds her love's body and she cries over it.

"What shall I do?" she asks me, but I have no magic answers for her, and I am gone. I leave her as the witch left me, alone and unsure.

By morning, I doubt if I did the right thing. Perhaps I should have allowed her ignorance, or perhaps I should have stayed to try to help her. Somehow, all I knew to do was to show what I had seen so that she could make her choice, just as I have made mine.

PATHWAY

I know not how to continue. If this is the way of the world of men, I doubt I will find my place inside it. I know I am lost. The wood is all around me and I feel it will never end unless I make up my mind to leave it. I have decided to head to the road and see if I cannot find a village or market town. I have a bit of food left, and wages from my last job. It might be interesting to see what men do with money.

THIS MORNING I find that I am nervous about approaching the road, as though it and not the wood is full of evil. But after all, it is just a road, leading to one place from another, stretching far beyond my eyesight. Many men have walked this road, and I would say a good many horses and chariots as well, so that it is not a narrow lane, but quite broad in my estimation. It must be an essential and well-used road, one that leads to a place where many like to travel.

I have not been this full of excitement since the night when I thought I would leave my tower. Thus far, my journey has been marked with tragedy and stories of odd, sorrowful people who are hurt—or whose aim is to hurt.

"That's all they are." I almost bite my tongue when I hear her disembodied voice come on the wind.

"What?"

Like always, my witch's worn voice leaves me chilled. "People. This is what I strove to shield you from, the problems of people. You've not had to see their misery; you've not had to walk through their wallowing degradation. You are more than they will ever be."

"I am more?"

"Yes, I have willed it and raised you to be more." I want to laugh at her delusion.

"I am less. I do not even know how to communicate with them. I am peculiar, separate from them. I've seen how they look at me."

"They are cruel."

"Sometimes, yes—but not to me. I have not received cruelty."

"Then you are fortunate, but you may not remain so." Her voice is now a wisp of smoke blown away. I cannot trace it and I will not follow it.

⌘

BEHIND ME, I hear a group approaching. They have a horse-drawn carriage, though it does not seem to me as fine as it is useful. I move to my right to let them pass, but instead they slow and stay a pace behind me. I chew on my apple thoughtfully. They are now moving about as slowly as I, and I wonder what game is being played. I hear a voice and realize I am being hailed by a few who have come up on the horses that were following along. Feeling unsure and quite ready to run back into the wood, I turn round.

"Hello, fair one! How have you come to walk our road?"

I turn back around and continue eating my apple. There seems to be no answer I can give them at this distance, and I will wait until they have caught up to continue what, I assume, will be an absurd conversation.

I hear a horse soon trotting up next to me and I look up at the rider expectantly.

"It is rude not to reply, fair one."

"How could you think me fair at such a distance, sir?"

"I could see it in your walk."

"Then you are perceptive indeed." I take a brief moment to squint at his outline, the sun making him a shadow to my eyes. I continue, noticing his horse is quite eager to recommence his former pace.

The man, however, will not be distracted. "Do you not know who we are?"

"I heard you say you are the owners of this road and I thank you for allowing me to use it." I don't know why, but I am put off by both his games and attention. I would that he would leave me alone.

"I am but a traveler, which makes this road mine."

"Then it is mine as well; I give you good day." I nod and try to dismiss him, but he keeps my pace. I see he is looking back at his comrades—though for support or what else, I know not.

I will put it to him plainly. "Sir, is there something you want of me?"

"Do you not remember who we are?"

I look at him as he reins his horse to stop and turn to me. The animal comes and begins to sniff me, but I am taken aback and trying to protect myself from the animal. Though I have now run into a few, horses are still overwhelming and I have never been perused by one. I had no idea their noses were soft as velvet.

The man laughs and reins in his horse from me. "Don't you like horses?"

"I've had too little dealings with them." I don't know by whom I am more disconcerted, him or his horse. I look into his face, shielding my eyes from the bright midday sun which had burned my vision before, keeping me from recognizing the troubadour.

I almost laugh at myself. "You are no sir; you are the lord's troubadour!" His face is darkened and lined by his travels, and he holds his horse with strength, his large gloved hands holding the reins to keep his horse to a walk.

"Not quite; I am my own, as are we all, just a traveling rabble heading from hearth to hearth to perform."

I do not know what to say. It is an awkward silence. He allows me to squirm in it.

"And where are you going now?"

"I should ask the same of you. A young maiden, traveling alone, aren't you afraid?"

"I have nothing to fear." I swallow, hoping this to be true.

"And your friend? What happened to her?" he questions.

"She gave you the end to her story, did she not?"

"Yes, the princess in disguise was found out, and we performed on her wedding day. She did miss her friend though, the one who had kept her secret so well."

"I am just a commoner, no reason to remain and scrub dish after dish when the world of men waits to be seen."

He looks as though he wants to laugh, "There is more to you than that."

"Am I a puzzle to be solved?"

"Indeed, and I will not be dismissed. Come, you must join us, at least until the next town."

Now, I know little of the ways of this world, but I do know that each person has a station in society, and these rebel players are not well-regarded in lofty circles because of their disregard for morality and odd way of living. While I was working for the Boar, one of the housemaids became quite familiar with a player. Roughskin told me that we could be friendly but must never give too much away to those beneath us. That maid was dismissed before I left the castle, and I suppose that a girl such as myself might never find a suitable position if she is thought to spend time with such men.

But then, how am I to learn if I spend all my time in solitude? And how can I refuse such a fascinating offer? Something in me is intrigued. I stand here, stilted, wondering how much I might regret either course of action.

"You hesitate. You wonder what people might think."

"Yes, and I also do not know you well. I am sorry," and

part of me aches to bend, "but I do not think it would be prudent."

"Ah, but to be prudent always . . . Well, there would be no songs for me to sing, no stories left, and the players would no longer play."

He is persuasive, but I am firm in my conviction that, though I might walk with them a ways, though I might talk with them, I cannot join them.

⚬⚬⚬

THE REST of the day drags, and though I pass one village, I buy some food and continue, without knowing why. When dusk begins to fall, I find my way into the wood to sleep—and there I see them, camped with a cheerful fire.

"How was your travel?" one player cries out to me on my approach.

"Long—and dusty, once your carriage passed me." They laugh at this.

"It needn't have been so," they take pleasure in reminding me.

I breathe in deeply, feeling a tinge of loneliness melt.

The night is full of autumn breezes that sweep over the flames, pulling and stretching them. I find myself staring into them, my eyes drying as I breathe in the smell of several kinds of wood as though intoxicated. I slow-blink. I am caught in their spell, the spell of storytelling. These are not stories to entertain courts or even captivate kitchen maids. No, they are twisted truths—some the players have lived through themselves, some that they have just heard of.

When one of the players begins a bawdier tale, I come out of my trance. I turn to the troubadour, who seems always close at hand. His skin has a flushed glow by the fire, with white crinkles where he has squinted and smiled into the sun. By the firelight, I can see he has removed his head covering. His hair is a sandy color and his eyes are very dark.

"How did you know Roughskin?"

His eyes smile, and he moves slightly, his back to the players, the fire at his right side. "I had met her before."

"Where?"

"In her father's kingdom, of course. But you knew that."

"Why should I know that?"

He leans into me, just a bit, but his intense gaze causes me to drop my own for a moment. His voice is baritone; it is easy to listen to, almost soothing.

"Because you know many things, and you don't accept what everyone claims as truth. You judge and determine for yourself; uncommon in women."

"Are you sure? Or perhaps you believe that because it was told to you."

"No. I've observed a great many women, and you are unusual. You have quite a story, don't you?"

"I don't know; the end has not been written yet." Why should I feel this comfort with him? Should I not be on guard? But even as I think these thoughts, I feel them slip away as ash, floating off to the starlit heaven above our canopy of trees.

"Where do you come from?"

I shake my head, trying to put him off. He is so good at

finding new stories, I am afraid he will have mine before morning.

"It is a simple enough question."

"One which you hope will lead onto others."

He nods, thinking. "I suppose that is true enough." He sighs. "Still, you can always refuse to answer more."

"I've refused now."

He studies me, head cocked, "Well, I know that you are not from these parts. Your speech, your mannerisms are all a bit alien."

"Then why ask?"

"Because I still don't know the exact place from whence you come . . . But I feel—"

I rise to my feet, not to startle him or seem rude, but because it is late. "I am sorry; I must find my place for the night."

"Stay with us!" I look at the players who have paused to invite me.

"No, you have no need for a woman, and I cannot sleep with so many men."

A crude remark is made, and the troubadour tries to lessen the impact. "Still, you may walk with us on the morrow. It will be nice to have you about until we reach our destination."

I don't ask them where they are going or why they should want me about. I don't want to think of them any more—I just want to leave. I feel unsettled, which alarms me, as mere moments before I had been comfortable.

The earth is cold after the pleasure of their fire, but I know that I am safer now, sleeping apart from them, than I would be in their midst.

PLAYING

It seems that players would sleep the day away if they could. Though they enjoy traveling the road, they only push ahead when hunger gnaws them on. Just now, these players are provided for and well-fed. From what I viewed last night, I believe their feasting will last perhaps a fortnight, but by then I heard them say they should be in a fine lord's province.

I got an early start, but by midday they had gained all the ground I'd made and asked me to break fast with them. I wanted to laugh, to tell them I had broken fast as morning crested the sky behind me—but there being no point, I said nothing.

I observed their strange family, how they cared for one another while still pushing and shoving each other in dramatic arguments. I wonder if all players act in such a way. They had on their best manners and tried to not touch the subject of women as best they could. They spoke instead of experiences, embarrassing moments on their blessed stage, of the different characters they loved to play.

I found it strange that two of them played all of the female roles. I could not believe that a man could do such a thing, convincing people that he was not a man, but a woman. They insisted that if I rode on with them, they would perform a short piece that evening.

I am now waiting for that performance. Why have I allowed myself to fall in with them? Why does it matter? Somehow, I feel it should, and I should resist—but it is too late. I have allowed myself to ride with them, though I am determined to still sleep apart.

⊂≈⊃

THE STORY UNFOLDS before me on the carriage that has opened into a stage. I see a girl, or at least she seems like a girl, sleeping. Her mother comes and wakes her. A great bear is waiting to take the girl away, giving money to her impoverished father as he takes away their daughter. The girl braves it as best she can and climbs on top of the bear's back.

The player who is the bear pretends to be galloping, and another player brings on a set piece to look like the cave where they will now live together. The bear is kind to the girl and she learns to love him. They play together in the day, but late at night, he leaves her. She tells the bear in the morning that someone comes to sleep beside her in the dark and she does not know who or what it is. The bear makes her swear to never tell anyone of this, but when he brings her back to visit her family, she tells her mother, who is scandalized. She gives the girl a small candle to light at night so that she can make sure it is not a hobgoblin or troll who has come to molest her. The girl, like a fool, obeys. She cries with delight—as do I—when she sees that a prince has joined her. The prince reveals that, at night, he is allowed to come out of a spell that makes him a bear by day.

The girl is enraptured as the prince begins to tell her of his enchantment, but then he shares that she could have freed him if she had just waited in darkness a year. As she cries, he leaves to accept his punishment from the wizard who cast the spell. All the girl knows now is that, on an island somewhere, her enchanted prince is bound to marry the wizard's odious daughter since he failed.

The girl is not put off; she calls to the wind for help. Four players surround her, dancing around with colorful scarves, pulling her this way and that. They pick her up, twisting and spinning her, but she will not give up. She begs them to be kind and help. One by one she asks them how to find the wizard's island where the prince is banished, but until she speaks to the West wind, she is lost. At last, the West wind carries her on his back until he collapses on the island.

I am in awe at how the players keep expanding the story, making the wooden stage that unfolded from their carriage change with their sheets of color. I feel like a child with one of my storybooks opening into a full picture before me.

The girl is plopped down, but at once she begs to see the prince. The wizard consents to let her see him at night, but the prince is asleep and she cannot wake him. The wizard drags her away but, after the girl begs, agrees to let her visit once more at night. This time, the girl sings to him, knowing that her song alone can break his new enchantment. The prince wakes up and sees the girl at last. The two escape together, this time carried by the East wind to live life together.

The players come on stage and I clap for them. Two of them step forward, take off their girlish wigs, and smile, that I might see the men beneath the play. I clap more loudly, impressed with their pretense.

⌘

IT IS morning now and I feel drunk, or something like it. I stayed up long into the night, discussing with the troubadour oddities in the kingdoms they have traveled. I asked questions, one after another spilling out of my mouth, a waterfall I could not dam. The boisterous players all fell asleep and I knew I should retreat, but the troubadour—there is something magnetic about our connection. He makes me feel that I should trust, that I should confide. I asked him why a father would want to marry his daughter. He said because the man was a fool. I asked him why a mother would bring a curse on her sons. He answered that she did not know the consequences of her actions. I kept asking things, things I didn't know, things I knew, but used the questions to learn what he knew. I searched and prodded, but I never asked him what I truly wanted to ask, things he could not answer.

Who is my mother? Where is she now?

Who is the witch? What made her a witch?

What of my father? Does he still live?

These are my questions, but the troubadour will never know. I find, to my surprise, that I wish he could.

❦

THE CARRIAGE CARRIES us through the next days. I begin to accustom myself to the players' ways, though I still sleep off by myself. I even asked if they would let me play the female's part, but they scoffed and replied that no woman is allowed as a player. They think it immoral. This strikes me as ironic, considering some of their lack of morals.

I believe the troubadour shelters me from some of their ways. I am grateful for his care.

"How long have you traveled with them?" I ask at night. The fire has lowered its height from earlier this evening. Darkness draws near as the wood glows.

He looks thoughtful. "Longer than I care to think."

"Did you always?"

He leans back. "No, I used to roam by myself, but this troupe makes an interesting showing. We offer a great deal others cannot. I like us very much."

"Then why is it, 'Longer than I care to think'?"

An owl hoots and then it swoops down; a small rodent tries to scurry away but loses its life with a screech. The fight is over quickly, though, and the hum of insects remains.

"What do you mean?"

"If you like your life, the one you have with the players, then why not think of the many wonderful years you have spent with them?"

"It is not the life I would have chosen for myself."

I wonder now: what makes a man a troubadour? What makes a man a player? What makes a man sing and tell of pain, of beauty, of stories he never lived?

"What is your story?" I hear a whisper in my voice.

He looks at me carefully, his dark eyes intense, guarding every thought. "It is too much for you."

"No, but you think it is too much for you. Who are you, sir?"

His laugh catches, and there seems a tinge of bitterness causing it to sound coarse. "You told me I am no sir, but a lord's troubadour."

"You told me I was wrong." There is a layer here I wish to peel back, but he shivers against the cold, he wants to guard himself against my questions. "You should not mind being questioned as you have questioned." I let things sit for a moment while he stares at me. "What is your story?"

"I have none." He turns away into the night, anguish in his voice.

⟨∞⟩

I JERK AWAKE, trembling in the cool air, unsure of where I am. I jump to my feet when I hear the hoot of an owl, but there is no other noise but the sound of the humming insects. I lower myself back to the ground and lay my head down. The darkness is lightening, but dawn is still a ways off. I pull my blankets tight around me in the grey that precedes the sunrise.

I've had a dream, this much I know, but it is oil-slick and I can't quite grasp it. I close my eyes in a haze and feel sleep beckon me to rest again. I remember something, and I jerk back up to a sitting position.

My love! I heard his voice, I saw his face! He was calling to me, reaching for me. He was in pain, music was screeching, his ears began to bleed, and he could no longer speak.

Suddenly, the troubadour stood before me, lute in hand, sneering at my love. Then, his face cleared and he turned to me, "Believe none of this," and he began to play once more, something that sounded like an eerie wind rising before a storm—the very sound the witch makes before I hear her speak to me.

"What am I to believe, if I cannot trust my own senses?" My dream-self had cried out.

"Nothing and no one," the troubadour laughed, and he sauntered away. I stared at Paul's face as he crumbled like a dried-out pot, becoming one with the earth.

ONWARD

"This is abrupt. Are you leaving so soon?" The troubadour's voice is at my back. I must have been preoccupied to not have heard his trudging through the thick carpet of leaves.

"Yes," I turn my head to face him, noticing he has not yet wrapped up his liripipe to cover his sandy hair. He comes to walk beside me, perhaps wondering why I won't slow my pace.

"You know the players will take a while to rouse."

"I must be on my way."

He catches my wrist with uncharacteristic force. "After all our hospitality, you spurn us like this?"

I look up into his darkened face. "I do not spurn you, sir, but I feel that I must move on now. If you are ready to go, then we may leave together, but I cannot stay here any longer."

He looks at me and releases his grip. "What has happened?"

"What do you mean?" I turn away from him and continue walking to the road.

"You are afraid. What have you to be afraid of?"

He will not be put off, and something in me longs to tell him, so I give a slight bend. "I've had a dream; I will not stay here to see it come true."

He pauses his stride. "You put much faith in dreams?" He waits and watches as I continue on. "I see you do—but tell me, fair one, why not wake us and warn us? Why not share that courtesy?"

"The dream does not bode ill for you."

"Then for whom does it bode ill?"

"Myself alone."

"And so you are leaving? Must you travel alone?"

"I don't know." I don't want to be alone. I've enjoyed his company, even though something inside me felt pulled by an undertow. He is following me again, and I am unsure of what to do. I stop and turn to him. "Please—I don't know what is best, only what is not. I cannot stay here a moment longer."

I begin to leave him, but he puts his hand, now gentle, on my shoulder. "Take this, you might need it."

I stare at the knife as though it is a snake.

"If you will not wait, take it."

I say nothing more, just close my eyes and take the weapon, hoping I need never use it. I turn my back once more and begin walking away. I am sure I will never see him again.

⚬⚬⚬

THE DAY IS long and windy. I curse my solitude and worry that my witch will come and speak with me while I am vulnerable. I have no way to defend myself against her wiles. Before I can contemplate long on this last fear, I see that the road is splitting. Without looking back, I know which road the players will take, so I take the opposite: the less used of the two.

◦∞∞◦

I ARRIVE at an inn after dusk and enter, though I feel uncertain. As I open the heavy door, I smell the sour ale in the steins and hear a few people eating and drinking. I feel rattled by their noise. My quick feet move over the hay-covered floor and I take a breath to steady myself. I go find the man in charge who is pouring ale at a nearby table. I ask both for a room and if he knows of any positions available for a young woman.

The lumpy, sweating man sets the ale's clay pitcher down with a thump. He rubs his scruffy chin, sizing me up for grit and capability. "I might. Inquire in the morning."

It is the most I will receive this evening, so I take my belongings to my quarters, a small room with bedding on the floor shared by myself and two women who have already settled down for the night. The room reeks of liniment, a smelly oil some rub themselves with before sleeping, as this discourages bed bugs. I wish I had arrived earlier; I would have looked with greater care at the bedding or walked back to the wood for the night. It is too late for such thoughts—I'll just bear it the best I can. I notice with a start how hungry I am, but now it is well into the night, too late for a young lady to be strolling about looking for food. I should have asked for a bite of bread before heading to my room, but I did not plan well. I am in a village now, and I must acclimate myself to what these people consider acceptable behavior for a young woman.

Am I acceptable? No. A girl without lineage, with a curse that might endanger any companion . . . A girl traveling alone, one who had even been in the company of players for a time . . . Yes, quite unacceptable, I'm sure.

But now I'm here and alone once more. I don't like the change.

⌘

THE NIGHT IS full of soggy dreams, of lutes drowning and the troubadour laughing. I turn to ask him what he is laughing about, but his friendly face distorts into that of the witch and I become a stone, cold and waiting in her darkness.

No longer sure if I am awake or still dreaming, I hear the wind rise, hear her scratching out her questions: "What do you think I should laugh about, little Rapunzel? You. You are quite funny—all of your escapades, all of your dreams of freedom."

I fight the cold stiffness that holds me immobile and manage to gasp, "Why do you taunt me?"

"Why did you leave me?" Her pain is tangible; I can hear the anger and fear in her voice.

"What are you afraid of?"

"Little girls who cannot identify their own fears should not inquire after others'."

I am sure I am awake now. Shaking my head, I snuggle back into my sheets, pretending that the rough bedding is both comfortable and sweet-smelling.

"What have you learned?"

"That I am not finished," I murmur into the darkness.

"Very well," she sighs. She appears before me, lit up like the moon. Her appearance seems younger and older at the same time, somehow more desperate. "Your lust will not be slaked, but this pursuit is empty. Finish it and return to me. Perhaps you will find me forgiving." She dissipates, and I rise to walk the room, careful to avoid waking the other sleepers.

The moon is still lighting the night. I have opened the windows, as I am too used to seeing it to feel happy indoors just yet.

I look out beyond me and see a great fortress in the distance. There is a tower attached to it, and I wonder who is imprisoned there. Perhaps no one—but to me, it seems that each tower has its captive, each castle a captor.

⁂

AFTER A BREAKFAST of hard biscuits and water, I set out to find the location told me by the proprietor at the inn. I am fortunate that he knew of something; I would have to wander on alone had he not.

"We are all alone," I remember my beloved saying one night. It seemed somewhat melancholy of him.

"What do you mean?"

"You seem to think that you are more alone than any other being, but it is not true. Every person is alone. You are cut off from civilization physically, which hinders you more than most—but you would be surprised to find how many people live more alone and more lonely than you."

"It is a common plight in the world of man, then?"

He had leaned back into his chair, his eyes looking away from mine into the fire, his right thumb rubbing the inner knuckle of his index finger. "It is the common plight of man. We must decide who we are and what we are to do. We must decide this on our own; no one can decide it for us."

I knew that he was speaking of some great decision he was making for himself, something he was still deciding, so I did not press. I wish now that I knew. It would give me more of him to hold onto.

I see the tower I noticed last night rising to the sky and I think about those who must have built it. Common people, like witches, spend their lives making and destroying things, envisioning dreams and nightmares alike. This tower—is it like mine, a nightmare enclosing a haunted soul? Or perhaps it is a tower, just a tower with no sinister purpose. It simply is.

As I stand in the grand entry, I find it strange that I should feel a chill while waiting to speak to the headmistress. Here it is though, along my spine, traveling up and down. My eyes roam to find an open door that is causing the draft, but all is still in the stone hallway. Upon my interview, I find that in the recent past the master has remarried, near harvest time. The halls have been social and happy since their union, but he will have to depart on business soon. Then the young mistress will be left to her own company, since much of the staff was a temporary gift as part of her dowry to transition her into her husband's new home.

I speak to the headmistress of my former positions, and something in her manner indicates an assessment made in an instant. Her judgment of my abilities is not verbalized. I am still unsure of my position in the household until the staff dines and I am allowed to sit closer to the middle of the table than the kitchen maids. Poor dears, I know how tiresome that job can be! The two girls, one fair-skinned and the other dark, seem to bear it quite well, though. They eat their meals just like everyone else.

The fortress is designed like most castles, up on a hill with turrets. It houses a wealthy family, though not a noble one, and therefore one with little enough need of an armory. Of course, the master employs a small guard who keeps his wealth safe as they travel with their various goods, but there are no true knights pledged to protect a lord and lady, and no land or peasants to care for. The dwelling is a massive, drafty place. After a few days go by, the master leaves with half the guard and several servants to see to his needs on the journey. It seems larger and draftier than ever, though I still cannot find the source of the current of air.

The mistress's name is Adeliza and she is not from this land. Her father is from the Northlands, and he settled nearby not long ago. He has three daughters, all of whom the master admired, but none of whom loved him. I asked the other maids who related the story why they should not, and they asked, had I never seen him? I replied I had not, and I was taken at once to see his portrait—quite a gruesome thing!—and I understood at once why any woman would loathe marrying such a man. But Adeliza did marry him. No one can explain this to me. Her sisters refused, but she changed her mind.

I've seen my new mistress at a distance, walking about the castle, singing in her soft way while opening doors, having candles brought in that she might examine all that she now possesses in her union. Could this be the source of her inducement? Or could her husband be wonderful beneath his wretched appearance? Even when I can't see

Adeliza, I know what she is about, lonely girl. She is comparing the life she used to have to the wealth she now possesses. I wonder if she is satisfied with her trade.

⚬⚬

"COME HERE, AND BRING YOUR CANDLE," Adeliza says with some authority, her words infused with an accent that reminds me of Paul. I am quick to come to her, tucking my rag away up the sleeve of my cotehardie. She hesitates a moment as we stand in the hall before a locked door. "Open it, please." She hands me the ring of keys with the correct one thrust forward.

I open the door and push it back as I make my way inside to light several other candles. As a servant, I should perhaps look away from my mistress's face, but I am nosy, so I watch as she searches for something. Her hair is black as midnight and her eyes are brown in a porcelain-white face that rests with grace on her neck. Her form is petite, accentuated by the loose tunic she wears with the sleeveless blue surcoat hanging over it, a beautiful black fur lining the bottom. Her eyes roam back and forth, each movement tinged with agitated curiosity.

I don't know what she is looking for, but there is something this room does not contain which she has determined she needs. Our eyes meet in that moment; I see the emptiness the arrangement has left her. She bows out of the room and I shut it up after blowing the light into darkness.

⚬⚬

THE HEADMISTRESS HAS CALLED me to her. She is a wiry old woman in an off-white cotehardie covered by a grey sideless surcoat. Her shoulders and back may be bent by age, but her grey eyes are sharp. Her hair is covered by a wimple, though I imagine it to be grey as well. "What did you say to the mistress?"

"Pardon?" I ask in bewilderment at her accusing tone.

Her face is a tight mask of wrinkles, earned over years of having to care for another's needs and wants. "The mistress seemed disturbed this afternoon and said that you didn't know your place. She is in the garden and wishes you to come to her."

"But——" I stop myself. There is no point in trying to defend myself here; I will only prove my impudence. "Of course. At once."

This beautiful place was built to show the master's magnificent estate. The small fortress boasts exquisite tapestries on its walls, the majority of which depict hunting scenes, and magnificent statues, which one might imagine had been commissioned recently. Outside its grand hall, there lies a beautiful, though dying, garden. A garden can be a cold place in the evening, but Adeliza often withdraws here, the servants say. It is one of the few places from which she can see her father's lands in the distance. Most of my journey after leaving the wood was such a gradual incline I hadn't noticed, but now I see how much higher we are. I see the valley covered by forestry, but I refocus my mind on the young woman before me.

"Mistress, you wished to see me?" I make certain that my eyes and head are lowered into the acceptable subservient position.

"Yes. You disturbed me this afternoon. I would like you to—" Her voice halts. "Why are you doing that?"

"Pardon?" I ask without looking up.

"I am speaking with you—please look up."

"I'm sorry," I say, at last raising my head.

"Who are you?"

"My name is Rapunzel."

"And whom have you served before us?"

"I was a maid twice before."

"I see. Not for very long, either." She pauses, but I don't comment. "You are as new to being a servant as I am to being a wife . . ." Her voice drifts off, losing its authority, sounding forlorn. The silence mounts as she gazes off again.

"Mistress," I interrupt after a long while, "what is it you wish of me?"

"Nothing. You may go."

"Yes, Mistress. I apologize for disturbing you earlier."

Her laugh is hollow, and something in her wistful countenance reminds me of Roughskin's regret for the life she had left behind. "It is not your fault. It is no one's."

∞

ADELIZA'S BEEN ROVING AROUND AGAIN today, her soft shoes shuffling while her skirts trail behind her. She is sifting through her keys, tossing a restless look at each door, sometimes stopping to open them, sometimes moving on. There is no purpose to her movements, and it seems she is lacking . . . what? I don't know. The master should soon be home;

perhaps it will cheer her, though I dread to see him in person.

⚬⚭⚬

THE MASTER HAS COME and gone again, leaving his wife behind once more. She seems fixated, yet listless. I see her approaching me, and I wish we were equals that I could offer her some comfort or word of advice. She need not stay in the fortress all day; I think it too depressing for her. She needs to be around others of her own kind, of her own age, outside and away from locked doors.

"Rapunzel?" Her voice sounds remote and I'm not sure whether I should look at her or continue with my work.

I compromise by stopping my work, but not looking at her. "Yes, Mistress?"

"Have you been up to the tower?"

My eyes shoot straight to hers though I can't speak a word.

"No one is allowed up there—not even the servants to clean it. Would you go with me if I asked you?"

I stare into her dark eyes, which seem larger than ever before. "I am your servant. Have you forbidden me?"

"It is the master who forbids it, not his mistress."

"If you asked, I would go." I don't know why I would. I can't imagine defying such a hideous creature, but I know that if she asked, I would.

She nods once and moves away.

"Why did you marry him?" My voice reverberates down the hall.

She turns to regard me. "You are impudent, aren't you?"

"I suppose I am."

She smiles a little. "I married him because my sisters wouldn't have him. I knew him in parties, I knew him in legend, I knew him a short time and I thought, *I want what he has*. This place, it possessed me from the moment I saw it. I longed to be its mistress, the keeper of its keys." She stops, mesmerized by something.

"And you are."

"No—it keeps me."

She is cryptic, her movements ghost-like, haunted by something she can't name, something she won't face.

I should let her walk away, I shouldn't ask anything more, but—"Why wouldn't your sisters have him?"

"They knew his legend as well, they had heard the fantastic stories—not that any of us believe them—but they wouldn't live with a man so . . . clouded. Only I would do that."

"What is in the tower?"

"No one knows."

"He has forbidden you to go there."

"Not exactly." In silence she moves away, leaving me to speculate what it is all about.

INVISIBLE

I might try to ask questions of the other servants, but few of them seem friendly. Most are drear, lifeless—and yet cynical. They only speak to repeat rumors and gossip. Not that one needs to speak all the time, but to say nothing without ceasing . . .? I should not complain; they could be loud and demanding. I remember the Boar. Perhaps I will look at this time as mending my ears from his noise. If only this place could be cheered.

I will stop thinking on this. It is my time to be out and away from duties. I am walking down to town when I hear of the nearby lord. He is quite a vain man, I am told, by another maid who is also out today. I have seen her before at the dining table, though we have spoken little as our duties never run us into one another.

"Is he quite powerful?"

"That depends on whom you ask, but none of his own servants seem to be able to defy him." Her face is bright, sparkling in the sunlight with her light grey eyes and honey-colored hair split into two braids and coiled over her ears.

"Then they are ideal servants, I suppose." We laugh at this and I feel the smudge on my spirit clear.

"What are you going to do while you are in town?" she smiles.

"I suppose I'll look around, have something to eat, perhaps find a place for my earnings." My clothing has been provided for, as the master likes all of his staff to wear the same drab colors. My earnings are quite a question to me. I look in happy expectation at her. I don't even know her name, and I've said more to her than anyone else in the past week.

She nods and suggests that we go to market together. I'm looking forward to comparing this one to the others I've seen. Roaming through it becomes a delightful though frightening experience. As I have discovered in other towns, one must always watch where one steps, for chickens, dogs, and cats roam around. There are droppings left behind by these smaller animals and evidence that larger ones have come through since the last rain. Stall after stall hawks their wares, shoving raw food and products into unsuspecting faces. I am always overwhelmed by the noise, the pushiness, and the mixed smell of feces, meat, bread, and people. My expressions seem to amuse the maid, whose name is Clarisse. I find out that she helps with the fowl my master keeps. She spends most of her time outdoors, unless it is to eat or sleep. She asks if I would like to join her family for dinner, and I find myself agreeing. I am taken aback by her generous nature, as though I am a stranger to any type of kindness.

"I cannot imagine working inside such a place," she confides as she purchases different foods for her family.

"But why not?" I ask, wishing someone to explain the melancholy curse of the place.

"Have you not met him? Is he not as horrid as they say?"

"I have not met my master, but I have seen his portrait—and there is no wonder that there are few mirrors in his castle."

"I don't think I could feel safe near him. Do you not know? They say he has murdered each of his wives."

I stare at her, forgetting the loaf of seed-crusted bread I was reaching for. "Has he had many?"

"To my knowledge, a great many. A dozen, at least, from different countries—and each disappeared, bodies never buried, children never born to carry out his line."

"But why should he kill his wives?" Of all the gossip repeated, this is the one story I have never heard. Are they all too frightened of the master?

"Though he has wealth now, they say he did not when he was young, and he determined in his heart to find wealth however he must."

"So he married and killed rich women?"

"That's what they say."

This seems ridiculous to me. "I don't understand."

At this moment a considerable ruckus begins and I hear some obnoxious horns blowing.

"Oh dear."

"What is it?"

"That is the sounding of the horns." She begins to move, but stops and continues her explanation at my blank expression. "Nobility is passing through the marketplace and we must step aside." She looks at me, bewildered, confused by my ignorance.

I follow the crowd and step aside, expecting a rather pompous chariot to pass by—but instead, I see that minions are escorting a man in the distance—a lord, I presume—in full view of everyone.

Upon seeing another of my bewildered expressions, Clarisse explains, "It is a lord. Some nobility like to allow us to—" she sighs as though she cannot find the right word "—gawk."

"At what?"

"Their—wealth, their superiority, their—" She stops with her mouth agape as the lord comes in full view. The entire marketplace is awash in silence; even the animals have gone mute at the sight of the lord prancing about in the cold without a thread on his bare body. He is smiling despite the cold, very much looking as though he is boasting his present condition. I overhear someone whisper something about the marvel of the lord's new clothing, and another echo the statement until almost all the voices are mingling with comments about the superiority of the lord's tailor, whom I am given to understand is walking near him, a wide smile stretching his mouth.

"But—" Clarisse grips my arm and I stop my statement and try to look away.

"Mother," I hear a child across the square, "the lord is naked!"

The mother looks devastated; I suppose she has not yet taught her son to not question the blatant stupidity of his superiors. I begin to laugh, first at the child, then at the mother, and then at the lord himself. Others cannot help themselves and join me. The lord is quite undone, taking a coat from one of his servants and beating the superior tailor who attempts to run off without success.

As the commotion clears, I have to catch myself before I fall over from laughing so hard, so we find a nearby bench and wipe our eyes.

"For a moment," she sighs, "I thought we were in trouble. If the others had not begun to laugh, it is certain we would have been."

"For laughing at a naked man who thought he was wearing, what, invisible clothing? Well, if I must be in trouble for that, then I must. But how could I not laugh?"

"You are unusual, Rapunzel."

"I know." I can feel my very oddness here, the way she is observing me, trying to understand my mind, trying to know why I am so different and naïve. She says nothing more, and we journey to her family's home at the far side of the village. The wood house even has a wood-shingled roof, unlike all the other thatch-roofed houses. The first thing you see when approaching is the forge that looks like a great trough of fire and the house built in behind it. The forge's back wall shares its great stone chimney with the house, though I can only imagine how much fuel they must burn for her father to shape the tools he makes. He nods at us while quenching a tool with a satisfying hiss in a barrel of oil before following us inside the one-room home.

❦

CHILDREN ARE PECULIAR. Clarisse is the oldest of her parent's children, of which they seem to have a countless number running about the long room among the hens and goats. The youngest are still at home, but I'm told many of the girls are working out, like Clarisse, and the boys help their father in the forge with his blacksmithing. Her mother is a petite, slender woman who has long honey hair without a hint of silver. She wears it in the fashion of ladies, braided and coiled on the sides of her head. I assume she covers it with a wimple when she leaves the house, but, busy lady, does she ever have time to leave her house except for Mass? She has a look of knowing about her that I would not dare to question. Clarisse seems to take after her father's stature; he is large and muscular, his face weathered by years and work, his hair the color of wheat, eyes black as night, teeth yellowed, but just a few missing. They are happy to meet me and guffaw at our market adventure, but the children don't seem to understand the joke.

"Why was he wearing no clothes?" her brother questions.

"Well, he must have thought he was."

"Oh! And it's been so cold today; he had to have felt it." Her mother tries not to laugh as she turns to swing out the bubbling cauldron from over the fire so she can stir the stew.

"Well, I'm sure he did."

"Then why didn't he put on some clothes?" the little boy continues to pester Clarisse.

Clarisse's father intervenes. "Because, Franz, he was

too proud. Like most nobles, he wanted the best of everything and was never, never satisfied."

"He was greedy?"

"Very, and so when the tailor could come up with nothing better than the best, I suppose he told the lord that he had made him a magical garment, one that only fools couldn't see. No one wanted to look the fool, so they pretended to see something that wasn't there."

"How do you know that, father?"

"You think I don't listen to what is spoken around the market? I hear what is said, and then I think on it and discover the truth as I pound out tools for other men. Pride is a great downfall of mankind.; we must always be careful to guard against it. It is one of the seven deadly sins."

This piques my interest; I want to hear more about sin, what it is and why seven of them, in particular, lead to death.

"Do you not remember Mass last Sunday when the priest spoke of pride and sloth?"

The young children nod their heads.

"We must be careful ourselves, lest we fall into such folly."

"Yes, and then we will be too stupid to realize we are naked," solemn Franz answers. I bend my head to smile; I would never want to embarrass the boy for understanding such a complex matter in such simple terms.

Clarisse's father just smiles and grunts. "Indeed. That would be very cold."

"Though it might be nice in the summer," Franz ponders.

"That is enough—we none of us will need to worry

about invisible clothing any longer. We have a guest, so perhaps we can find something else to discuss. Marta, why don't you show Rapunzel where she can sit by Clarisse?"

The little girl takes my hand in her soft one and leads me to sit on the creaking, narrow bench while everyone finds their place. They thank the Host, who is said to be the Spirit of God, for their food, and begin to eat.

I feel warm listening to them catch up with one another during and after the meal, and though I do not join in, I feel somehow part of their celebration. Each of them is connected, not by work nor by mere blood, but by their care for each other. Their home feels lighter than almost anywhere I've ever been, though it is plain and crowded. I marvel that even with so many children, there is only this one room, a great room where the family lives and eats, and the parents sleep with their children in a long bed. Sharing their home with their animals, I am at a loss. Surely there is never a quiet moment to sit down alone in this place, but they all seem happy and well-fed. I am not allowed to leave without accepting a bundle of food and a promise to return next fortnight on my free day.

⁂

As we walk back up the incline toward the fortress, I notice Clarisse is quiet.

"What is wrong?" I inquire—for I feel that something must be.

"Nothing." Her shoulders give a slight shrug as she shuffles her feet forward. "I enjoy my family and wish to begin my own. My mother was a maid before she married my father; there is no shame in it. I just have to be patient."

I want to ask her how she knows she will have her own family. How does she know she will find someone she wants to share her life with? I don't know her well enough to ask any of this, though.

"What of you, Rapunzel? Has a young man picked you out?" She smiles into my eyes, but it falters. "I'm sorry. Are you quite well?"

I nod in silence and look away.

"I—I—"

I force myself to look at her again. "It's not your fault. You didn't know." I lick my chapping lips. "I did want a family, but I don't feel I know what one is. Now, I just want . . ."

There is nothing more to say. Our parting is not awkward, though it seems that it should be after such a strange conversation. We hope to meet again in a fortnight, and late that night as I lie in bed hearing the other house-maids' peaceful breathing, I wonder why I met her—and why she was so kind to a stranger.

BEHIND THE DOOR

*J*hear the doors opening and shutting in random succession. Who are they trying to let in, where do they lead, and what are they shutting off? Ridiculous questions spread their tentacles throughout my mind as I lie down to sleep in the housemaid's quarters at night. I hear them and I wonder. My mistress seems to grow sicker daily, her wandering about the halls through the wings more oblivious, as she never sees what is in front of her. Her mind is always gazing at what is behind her, the door she dares not open. The doors she does open, they open and shut their smacking mouths, mocking her debilitated state.

I noticed, soon after my day off, her wan complexion. She seemed weary, though she rallied the next time the master was home. Once he was gone again, though, she couldn't seem to concentrate, and weeks went by with her eating little to nothing, face greying, rarely going outside even to gaze at her father's castle.

I've become accustomed to hearing her drag her feet

back and forth as she sifts through the keys, letting them ring and clink in contradiction to our hush. For we household servants are silent about her; we don't know what to say. Not even her personal maid knows what to say, and I wonder if the young bride, though she is a grand mistress in her right, is dying a little from solitude. It sounds like something that could not happen except in the books the witch took from me—but Adeliza seems so alone, so tired. I wish I were her equal so that I could talk to her with the same freedom as she has with me.

My work is like it was before—routine, though I find satisfaction in how I do it. I wish Clarisse was a housemaid so that I could have someone to confide in, someone to listen to. I speak to her on our days off, but she does not know what to do for our mistress any more than I.

◌⁑◌

ADELIZA IS WITH CHILD. I can tell now. Though she has been with the master for such a short time, I confess that once I had the thought she might be, somehow it made sense. I am now wondering if there is a way I could broach the subject with her, though I may have to look for another post soon after if she is offended.

My chance is not long in coming, as later this same morning I see her walking towards the latticed window I am cleaning. This is promising, since she has not looked outside once in recent days. There is no other person in the corridor and I cast her a curious glance, hoping that she will take notice of me before I need to speak.

Her eyes drift over the landscape, giving the impression

of one who is looking but not seeing. She is not going to speak, but she is aware of me and I decide to rely on chance.

"What are you looking for?"

A slight smile curves her lips. "Life," she replies without glancing towards me.

The light silence lies between us now and I continue my work without interrupting her search—for now, she does appear to be both looking and seeing.

She gives her head a slight turn in my direction, her long dark hair pulled back into an intricate weave at the back of her neck, cascading over her burgundy surcoat. "What do you look for?"

"I don't know that I look for anything."

"Yes you do—you are looking for something."

I pause in my work. "I don't know that I can name it."

She nods and turns back to the window. "Yes, it is hard, isn't it, Rapunzel?"

The question is similar to what the witch had asked me —but it feels so different that I feel myself yield, "Love." But it doesn't sound true. "Answers."

"You search for answers? I see. But what questions do you ask?"

I hesitate, sensing my opportunity. "Why are you afraid?"

Her eyelids flutter and close down, moths resisting the flame, but they cannot stay closed long and her dark eyes hold me. "He will find me. And he will kill me." Her delicate white hands smooth the green velvet fabric down over her abdomen, leaving it darker than the rest of the material.

"Why should he want to kill the mother of his child?"

Her mouth forms a question though her voice is still.

"Are you not with child, my lady?"

"I am, but—"

I shrug.

At once her eyes seem relieved and then they grow determined. "Finish what you are doing here and come find me. I will be in my bedchamber."

I nod, wondering if I have just said too much.

After completing the windows in the hall, I find her looking pale and resolute, holding a beautiful mirror before her. She speaks before I have finished shutting the massive door.

"If you have stomach, I have something on which to feast." Her gentle hands lay the mirror down and she rises from her seat. "There is a key I have not used. What use is it if I do not? Will you go?"

She has not looked at me since I entered. I bow in submission and wait to follow her, but she does not head to the door. Instead, she walks to a tapestry and beckons me to come.

"Lift the corner," she instructs, and as I do I see the first door we are to open. It is unlocked—though, I gather from its screeching hinges, not much used.

She nods to me and I carry the light before us, leading up the stairs to the door she has never opened. I assume that we are using a discreet passage because she does not wish for the other servants to know what we are about. She stops beside me on the landing and fiddles with her ring before sorting through her keys. I am sure she knows which one she wants, but she looks at them all. Is her desperation great enough to discover what is behind the door ahead? She cannot linger long; her obsession is too much for that.

It gives way with ease. An intake of breath sounds as she opens it, and I feel a frigid chill, though there is no opening to the outside. In a moment, we can see nothing in the dimness until I lift the light to illumine what is within.

Women are dangling by their hair, frozen screams on their lips, some of their bodies marble white while others are tan and brown, one nearly black as night. There are women made differently than I have ever seen before. They are hanging still, though it feels that they are swaying back and forth. I realize it is I. I am swaying—and, by accident, I catch myself when I reach out and touch one of them. A sharp scream claws the air, but it is not from me or Bluebeard's dead wives, but from his live one who drops the keys to the sticky floor. There should be a wretched smell, but there is not. There should be a sound, for the wives look as though they wish to speak—but their eyes do not meet my own: they meet hers. They warn her, they plead with her, and they shriek unspoken threats to make her leave.

"We should not have come here." I don't know which of us said it, but we leave the chamber of wives behind, their unclosed eyes having told us more than we wished to know.

"He is coming, he is coming—" Her screeching voice is full of terror, of pain as she tries to run and trips down the stairs and passage. "I must leave here, I must go. He mustn't find me, not now, not when . . ." But the key she holds is stained. While she erratically packs her bags, I try to wash off the offending stain and find that it will not come clean. The blood has turned black on the key, leaving no texture, but it will not be washed free of the taint.

"It won't come off," I mumble, perplexed and afraid. It is the one rational thing I can think of doing, to try to remove the fear by taking care of the blood.

"My ring!" Her voice shocks me with its volume and I turn away from the washbasin at once to see her collapsed on her bed among her things.

Grand ladies often wear their heavy clothing too thick to remain cool during extenuating circumstances, so I rush to dampen her face and revive her. She gives a dull shake of her head and beseeches me with her eyes. "It clouded last night; I thought it was the child. But now, I have seen what he did not want me to see. I will join them before the night is over."

She lifts her trembling hand and shows me her ring, the one that she twisted when she wasn't sorting through her keys. It is indeed a darker color than it had been before—but what does that have to do with his returning to kill her? Is this madness? How can one resign oneself to being murdered by an absentee husband? "You will not join them," my voice is harsh. "You have a child within you. Even if the father is a monster, you will see that child born. Now, we will leave and he will not find you—or if he does, he will find out what happens to monsters that kill their wives."

She is not listening as I set her on her feet again and shove her out the door. "The priest said he might mean me ill and to take the ring. It has turned black. He is already here, Rapunzel, and I have done two things I should never have done."

These stupid grand women, jabbering when they should make their legs run. I venture no further conversation with her and I almost tear her arm off as we make flight down the hills before us.

"He will find us. The ring says he is near." Her voice becomes more grating as I make her run.

"Tell the ring it is wrong, or that it can stay to meet him. We are going elsewhere, and he will not find us."

"When he kills me, tell my father . . ."

She begins rambling some absurd speech of woe to relate to each member of her immediate family but I take no heed. I am not a messenger. I was not much of a maid until now, and I suppose I could learn the trade—but who would want to hear the message of a person who might have saved the life of your kinsmen if they had traveled faster? Soon, her speaking becomes faulty; she is running out of breath as we have come to the copse of trees that will carry us behind the market. I am grateful for this small miracle as I push ahead, hoping that my sense of direction will not fail us.

FLIGHT

It is not yet evening when we reach our destination. I knock at the back of the house with trepidation, hoping that I am right to come here. Clarisse opens the door, to my surprise and her own.

"Rapunzel! What brings you here?"

Out of breath and fatigued, I wonder how much I should say. "Our mistress needs help. I knew of nowhere else to turn." I look back at Adeliza. At this moment, she seems a girl—small, young, and quite helpless.

A flicker of concern crosses Clarisse's brow, but she opens the door wide and invites us inside. "My mother took ill a week ago, so I have come home to help."

"I am so sorry, we do not wish to be a burden. I have money I can pay . . ." I pat the small lump I keep tied beneath my garments, as I never know when my restless feet will make me leave a place.

"Oh no, please do not concern yourself with money. My family will be honored to take care of our mistress—and yourself, of course. I only wish we could—"

A soft groan interrupts Clarisse's tale, and she turns to tend to her mother and another sibling who also seems unwell.

Adeliza seems peaked, and I make her sit on the bench at their table while I get her some watered ale. She looks distant and her skin is warm to the touch. I wonder if she is getting ill again. She soon excuses herself and returns trembling, having relieved her stomach of whatever ailment was bothering her.

She gathers her bearings as she looks about the large room. Of course, it is not a large room such as she would be used to seeing, and she stares in astonishment at the children as they filter in for the evening meal that Clarisse has been finishing.

As I set the stale bread, trenchers, and two knives on the table, I wonder what kind of impression it is making on Adeliza. Smiling, I ask her of her health.

"I am feeling better, thank you." She looks at Clarisse with unmasked curiosity, "Did Rapunzel call you Clarisse?"

"Yes, it was my grandmother's name."

Adeliza smiles. "And my mother's, before she died—but we are not from here. What is your mother's name?"

"My mother is Melisende and her people are from the Northlands, but my father's people—"

"What about me?" her father's great, booming voice roars as he enters the house. "I see Rapunzel has found her way back with—" But his cheerfulness drops off into confusion as he gazes at Adeliza.

"You must be the master of the house," she smiles with benevolence, a graceful bearing few could learn. "Your daughter has allowed us to come in when there was nowhere else for us to go."

He nods, a soundless sign that he might ask more at a later time when little ears are sleeping.

☙❧

"Who is your master?" He asks without ceremony once the children are settled and on the other side of consciousness. He directs the question at me, but Adeliza will not have me speak on her behalf.

"The people call him Bluebeard, and I am sure you have heard all the tales of his many wives."

"I have heard that he has had many wives and no heir. Why have you left his protection?" I can tell now that he is trying to decide if, in truth, he should board us; is it the right, proper thing to do?

She holds out the bloodied key and he crosses himself, seeing it as an emblem for evil. "On our wedding day, he gave me the keys to his house and told me that I might roam at will. Of course, he said, there might be doors that I opened that I might never be able to shut again. I had heard the tales, the stories of what might have happened to dozens of wives from this land and the other lands he came from. My sisters would not have him because of the stories; they told me I was touched if I did. But I paid no heed. I was obsessed with his fortress—" her confession jars her, and she shakes her head at her greed "—I wanted it, you see. And so I had it and the man; but now, I have seen behind all the doors, and the stories are indeed true."

He contemplates, his head nodding without him

knowing as he digests all she has said and not said, determining within himself how much more he needs to hear. His large hand combs his beard in rhythm, until at last it stops and he looks back at her. "He means you harm?"

Melisende joins us, though her husband tries to shoo her back to bed. "Gotfrid, I cannot sleep any longer, please let me join you. My nights are my days now. Besides, I am feeling well enough to find out what great lady we have in our home." She looks a ghost in her white shift, and her husband cuddles her in his lap.

From her finger Adeliza wriggles off the ring she had been moaning about earlier and stares at it. "Before I left my father's house, our priest gave me this ring to know my husband's intentions. As long as it was clear, he said, I would be safe. A few days ago, I learnt I was with child, and I knew I had to find what was behind the last door, the one in the tower that no servant ventured near. The ring had begun to cloud and I made Rapunzel go with—"

"She asked and I consented," I correct.

"Rapunzel came with me and saw as well, the wives all . . . hanging from their . . . hair . . . and the floors . . . covered . . ." Her eyes begin to film over again, and I reach over to try to pull her back, catching the ring before it falls on the hay-covered floor.

"So, you see—we had to leave." I finish.

"I suppose we could have gone to my father's," her voice lowers.

"He will look for you there first. Melisende and I quarreled early on in our marriage, right before Clarisse was born, and it was the first place I looked for her. Found her crying on her mother's lap at her father's hearth." His eyes warm at the memory. Clarisse smirks, entertained by the thought of her parents so young and inexperienced.

The moment moves forward and I must ask them: "Are we to stay here tonight? Would you rather we go?"

"If you are not afraid of becoming ill," the pale ghost smiles, "you should stay the night. We will find the right place for you on the morrow. Tell me, did anyone take notice of you in the marketplace?"

"We came through behind. I did not want to chance meeting him on the road and wanted to avoid as many people as possible."

"You are a smart girl, Rapunzel. You have served your mistress well." He takes a great breath. "And now let us find you bedding on which to sleep."

Soon the matter is settled, with Clarisse and me on the hearth with blankets, Adeliza on the best straw covered in thick blankets. I find sleep a mercy as it is dreamless, and I awake hoping that Adeliza was spared the same as I.

⋯⋯

SOMETIME BEFORE THE break of day, Clarisse's father consulted their priest and obtained some right of passage for the two of us to a nearby convent. Though I am not her personal maid, my rescuing her has raised my status, and I am to accompany her and see her settled in before journeying to leave word with her family of her whereabouts. Perhaps I am to learn the trade of message-bearing after all.

⋯⋯

A CONVENT IS QUITE a peculiar place. In particular, it is a strange one for ladies to give birth in, considering none of the nuns themselves will ever know men or marriage or children. Still, it is cloistered and safe, a haven for one so battered, and I hope it will mend Adeliza as she dwells within its walls. As for myself, I know that I have a great deal to learn about their religion, of which I know practically nothing, and I feel a wisp of curiosity about the many months ahead.

Though another messenger is offered, Adeliza insists again that I go, but that I also return to her. Somehow she has attached her own sense of safety to me, staring at the odious ring day and night, grateful that it is no longer black, wary that it has not cleared.

I am weary of traveling, but I know that I must leave soon. It will take several days to reach her family's land, as my way will not be direct and I must go on foot. I look forward to being out again, but I do not know what awaits me.

THE WAY FORWARD

The air has grown cold since my first solitary weeks of journeying outside. If not for the message in my breast I would not continue—but the November chill does not break me; I refuse to give into its fears and worries. My feet continue to tread the hard ground, my endless steps grinding the dirt beneath me. I keep to the road, knowing I will lose my way otherwise, but I am wary for sounds of those approaching in case Bluebeard is looking for us. I shake away the image. My mistress is safe from her lord, and I will reassure her family.

These thoughts have comforted me over the last several days of cold. Each footstep seems lighter, for the way I go helps another, someone outside of me. I am again alone with my thoughts, and I wonder about the future after Adeliza has her child—where will she go? It seems that the nuns would be content to allow her to become one of their own, but would she be suited for such a closed life? Their pallets are hard, their meals coarse, their cloaks heavy to wear. I know that her life has had none of these elements, a girl who became obsessed with a grand fortress and all its possessions. Of course, she might be cured of it now—I know not.

Tonight is the coldest by far, and I dread to think of how much colder it will be on my return. I see a small cottage ahead and I am tempted to stop there, to get out of the wind—but I hesitate, wondering what strange and horrible things I might encounter. One might just as well say that I may encounter such things outside, but at least here I can run, so I choose the wind that drives me.

◌◦◦◦◦

THE NEXT MORNING finds me in another meditative frame of mind. *Perhaps this is what it feels like to be old . . .* My thoughts drift as the dawn never breaks through the clouds, the sky a mottled grey. I wait for the incoming snow.

I sense her before I see her: my witch's presence is as tangible, as evil as the whipping wind that brings her.

"How are you, my child?" Her form is that of a peasant woman, traveling alongside, matching my stride, though her manner is older than mine. Her back is bent with age and her gait unsteady, halting steps that I don't wish to accommodate, knowing it to be a charade.

I debate within myself whether to answer. Does conversing with her increase her hold on me? "Quite well."

"I see; traveling through the cold, for a girl you know but little, to protect her from her brutish husband—this makes you well? Interesting choice."

"Do you think so?" I focus on a small group of birch trees, their claw-like limbs stripped bare of leaves, reaching up to the darkening sky.

"Yes, of course, I have always been fascinated by those who choose to serve others when they could instead live for themselves."

"She would be hanging by her hair at this point, both she and the child dead."

"The child was not yet born and is of no relation to you—why should you care? If its own father doesn't want it—"

"Its mother does."

"Did you ask her?" I can hear her fiendish smile though I stare at the ground, searching for rocks that might trip me.

"I want the child if she does not."

"You would take her child?"

"Not from her, but if she did not—"

"I see. You think you could be a good mother, though you reject the only one you've ever known." Her tone accuses and she stops still. I feel the heat from her gaze as I try to keep walking.

"I don't know that I would be a good mother."

"Well, but you'd like to try."

I stop and make myself turn to face her apparition. "I'd like to have a family of my own, yes."

"Yet no matter where you go, you leave, never remaining, never finding a husband, and never making a home." She lets this obvious truth settle on me, hoping for some reaction, I suppose. "Why won't you settle, Rapunzel?"

"I don't know how." It's a bitter thing to say, but nothing she does not already recognize. "Why do you keep coming to find me?"

"I'm curious," her voice rasps in pain. She takes half a faulty step forward, straightening her back. "I want to see what you see. Perhaps you'll find something in this world that I never did. Perhaps I was wrong for shutting you away."

I look over at her, seeing the witch beneath her peasant garb. She is still sharp and withered, coveting all she dares not touch. "You don't believe that."

"But you do," she hurls, her jagged words jarring me as her peasant-image melts away into its true form. I turn away and resume my former pace. I hear her steps pursue me as she screeches. "My own child, my *lone* child believes I did her wrong, and I want her to know that I did the one thing that I could. I was trying to save you from all of this!"

"Are you certain your concern was me?" I toss over my shoulder.

"Explain your meaning."

I blink, swallowing her bitterness. I try to piece the words and phrases together, but nothing makes the sense I want it to. I am left with a deep void, one that might mean nothing to her. "You felt the pain of a world that rejected you—perhaps you did want to shield me from that, but weren't you also afraid that I might reject you for that world?"

"Simpering fool, you think it's that simple?"

She has caught up with me now, and I turn to look at her as I continue to walk. "Isn't everything?"

"No, you have a great deal more to learn in this *lovely* world. Keep running; you will never be satisfied!" And she is gone, but the wind seems calmer for her leaving.

BLUEBEARD

I wait outside the massive doors to the fortified dwelling for a short time, stamping in the new snow to keep my feet warm. The door is opened and I am ushered in, where inquiries are made as to my personage and business. I say simply that I have a message for the master and refuse to speak to anyone else, no matter how insistent they seem.

At last, I am joined by the headmistress. She is an older woman with blue eyes and a firm mouth—protective, I believe.

"What is it you have?" Her speech is direct, but she tries to smile, to invite me to share.

"A message I must deliver to the master alone, as I have said before."

Her blue eyes narrow, but she motions for me to follow her to a large frigid hall where the master joins us at last. She does not bow herself out, and I wonder how close her connection is with the family. The master is a slight man, though tall, his hair greying at the temples.

He squints as he looks at me with dark eyes that remind me of Adeliza.

"Sir, thank you for seeing me. I am to inform you that your daughter is safe and well."

His dark grey eyebrows come together in puzzlement and he speaks with a thick accent like Adeliza's. "Who are you to inform me about my daughter?"

"Her servant, Rapunzel. She instructed that I first speak to you, that I might reassure you of her safety and well-being." I stop lamely, misgiving heavy on my heart.

"I would assume she would be well in her husband's house. Is she lonely and sending for her sisters to come visit?"

"No, she does not wish her sisters to visit at present, but she begs that in the future—" I stop, feeling almost as though I can smell something dark. And yet it is not a smell —it's almost a lack of smell. I stare at the master and then around me, at the entirety of the well-lit room. The fire burning in peace should be warm, and a few candles are lit around the spacious hall, revealing scenic tapestries hanging from the walls, colors vibrant and woven thick, family emblems, ornamental relics resting on a bulky mahogany table . . . But something is wrong.

"In the future?" He smiles at me to encourage me to finish, but my feet begin to back towards the door. His smile is false, his words untrue. The firelight is a lie and blinks as he tries to reach me. "Rapunzel?" But I've heard that voice before. It spoke Adeliza's name in a husky, low tone the one time I saw him. There is no softness in it now, mere urgency, and a growing desperation. "Where has she gone?" The image of Adeliza's father still speaks, but it is

Bluebeard's voice I now hear; all pretense of a Northland accent vanishes.

I turn, knowing I must see a way to escape this mirage, but before me the apparition of the firm housekeeper blocks my path. Her cruel face smiles into mine, "Where has she gone, Rapunzel? What has she seen?" Her voice, too, is Bluebeard's.

I hold my breath, fearing that I might breathe in the evil about me. The light is now fading, revealing the cold blue of reality; all of the rooms are unlit, but not wholly dark. Bluebeard's sorcery no longer keeps up the façade, and both images disappear as his true form looms before me in its monstrous horror.

"You must tell me now!" he roars, lunging with his great hands at my throat.

I must be slippery, for I manage to evade his grasp, stepping backward and somehow winding my way out of the tangled tunnels the castle seems to be. Always at my back, I hear him growling, "Rapunzel, where has she gone? I must know where my wife is!"

I am running out of the mouth of a cave, and the cold air sears my lungs as I beat the ground with my feet. I cannot return to the convent—not until I know he no longer hunts me.

It is a wretched game. I hear him coming and I cower in different hiding places, waiting for him to pass, but he knows when I run again. He will not give up the pursuit. I try to master my fear, to control my breathing lest my panting give away my whereabouts.

I chew on the new snow, hoping to chill my breath and match the air. I can see his own breath long before I see him, and I know that he has almost found me again. I mask myself as best I can, knowing some of what he is capable of, imagining what he might do to find her.

"Is she near?" he calls out. "Will she not love her own husband anymore? She looked behind the door, did she not, Rapunzel? You knew it a foolish thing to do—why not stop her? We would have gone on happy, free. She needn't have known what happened before; it needn't have affected our love." His voice is drifting away. I am tempted to sigh in relief, but I resist the urge, knowing I must gather the courage to lead him still further away from her, further into the uneven terrain.

A hand grabs my throat and pushes me to the ground. I can smell him now, the cold, iron smell of death breathing into my nostrils. "Where is she now?"

"Outside your grasp," I choke.

I mask my emotions as I try to think how to wriggle out of his hold, but I am afraid, for he would think nothing of killing me, leaving my body to freeze as he goes to collect another wife for his chamber.

"Tell me what I want to know." He releases the pressure around my neck without letting go.

"I cannot." I focus on his ugly face and wonder what makes it so grotesque. There is an unquenched lust behind it, worked into every crevice, every line, and every tint of his blotchy skin.

His beard brushes me as he nears my face, and I strain to not writhe or gag. "You will tell me—I must have her back."

"To kill her?"

"To kill our child." The hatred in his eyes, the abandonment of compassion or understanding holds me in its icy grip, and though he is a great many times larger than I am, I determine I must get away to make sure her child is indeed safe.

I exaggerate my pain as I shut my eyes, trying to make him believe that I am willing to surrender to his power— but I'm quick to pull out the knife I keep hidden inside my cloak and pray it is sharp enough to pierce through his coat of thick skins. He yelps in surprise, but I know it is not a mortal wound so I bounce away as quickly as possible, running up in a direction toward which I feel a pull. My body snaps to a stop at the edge of a cliff, and I quickly flatten myself, hugging the ground. Too late he sees me, and Bluebeard slips in the snow. His body sails over, landing below with a horrible thud.

I watch, but no sign of life emerges. I sit down, winded. It is impossible. Impossible he should have found me, impossible he should have had me, that he should have fallen. Impossible—but that is what has happened.

I pick my way through the fallen snow again in dumb silence. I must find her father's real castle; she will want to know if the monster killed her family or if they are well.

◌⊃⊂◌

THE REMAINDER of my trip is uneventful, but her family is hungry to have Adeliza back safe and sound after the child is born. One of her sisters, Mary, insists on accompanying me on my return trip, and since the leather of my shoes has worn thin, I enjoy the plush carriage we ride in. I suppose I should have insisted on staying on the top by the coachman, but they all seem to think me her personal maid—and I suppose, by this point, I am.

We arrive at the convent but a fortnight after I left it. Of course, everything seems dull and stale after being nearly strangled by Bluebeard. I wear a scarf around my neck to hide the purple bruises that are slowly turning brown. Adeliza's sober form absorbs the story and leaves the room for a short time. Mary pats my hand as I anxiously await her return. Mary is wise, it seems, for when Adeliza returns, she is more composed and able to greet her sister with joy, though her eyes are puffy and pink. In the first weeks of December, she blossoms and smiles, all the while reminding the nuns of the beautiful things that will happen come Christ Mass.

Though the weather is not so wretched to keep Adeliza from returning to her father's house, it is thought best that she spends her time in waiting here—and, in fact, that she leave the child here once it is born. I don't quite understand all of it, but they promise to try to explain it all to me over time.

IN BETWEEN

*I*t's been interesting to watch the changes in Adeliza as her slight figure rounds. Though Mary and the sisters try to keep her inside and sedate, to calm every anxiety by serving her, she wrestles with the need to run about and dream. It is strange considering the origin of her child, but she seems free of her greatest fear and devoid of all concerns about leaving this child in the hands of the Church for training. She is not the somber, depressed creature I once served, but a strangely carefree girl.

Today the snow was irresistible, and while the nuns were in the chapel at prayer again, we bundled up and went to frolic about. Adeliza's pale face flushes as we tramp further and further into the snow, just beyond the cloistered walls.

"Remember when we were young and would do this?" she smiles to Mary, memories fresh in her eyes. "We would put on our warmest clothes and go outside just to run."

"Well, I don't know that you can right now." I smile at

her form. Though it is not as round as they say it will get, she has surprised me in how she has begun to fill out, now that she no longer becomes ill in the mornings.

She laughs without reserve. "I know! I remember a maid of mine having her first child. She had to stay at home as her time went along—her ankles swelled up to the size of two barrels." She stops and looks at me. "I felt the child move yesterday." The wind tugs but cannot dislodge the snug hood upon her head. "It was the strangest sensation, two little bumps, like small bubbles, right here," she indicates by tapping on her stomach. "I think I held my breath for almost an hour afterward, wanting to feel it again, wanting to know what this child is like. They say it is too soon to feel the child, but I did."

I suppose my question is too personal, quite invasive of a servant to ask her mistress—but I feel much more than her mere servant; I have been her protector and confidant. "Will you be able to give up the child, then?"

"Of course she'll give the child up," Mary says, coming round and putting her arm around her sister.

"Yes. It is only right. I thought I should hate this child, but I don't. Neither can I carry this small one with me back to my father's home. In this world, my child cannot be anything but the child of a monster, a thing to be scorned or feared. But in there—" Adeliza looks back at the way we have come "—this baby will be a child of God, a servant of the Church. My father will provide the dowry for the child to enter as a novice, and the Church will care for the child."

I want to nod in understanding, I know that many noble families dedicate one of their children into the work of the Church, but for the child to have its fate already settled even before it is born, for it to be known that this child will never have a chance at any other life . . . My eyes falter and I cannot look at her. This is not my world and I do not understand.

The young women begin chattering in heated anticipation again about the Mass that is to come at the end of this new month. I know that I should listen and try to understand the story of the celebration, but I cannot focus my mind, so the festivity becomes a blur to me. The nuns typically commemorate the Mass with all due piety, but with the girls here I can tell that this Christ Mass will be a bit more exciting than all the previous ones celebrated in their convent.

⸎

ALSO CALLED AN ABBEY, the convent is made up of numerous small dwellings in a clearing. North of the convent rests a hill which protects it from the coldest of winds, and a man-made wall of stone encloses all but one of the wood buildings. This building is called the oratory, a house for any male visitors—in particular, the abbot who visits a few times a year. He comes as an "extraordinary" confessor, to allow the nuns to unburden their consciences and also express any insights for change that they might not feel at liberty to share with the abbess. I've been told that the abbot's next visit will be soon, in time for the grand celebration, and I find myself curious about what his visit will bring.

Inside the protective wall are five buildings situated

around a dirt yard. On the south is the infirmary, which at present has no patients—and for that we are grateful. Still, one of the nuns, Sister Agnes, cleans it out every week, keeping it stocked with fresh linens and healing herbs so that she will be ready if the need arises. The building northeast of the infirmary houses the kitchen, storage cellar, and the refectory where we eat our meals in near silence as a novice enlightens us with readings. From the readings, I find I am learning more and more about what these people believe, but I still seem at a loss to their customs, fumbling when eyes are upon me.

Further north is a garden and orchard that provide sustenance for this small community. Next to this is a workhouse and stables, where there are two goats, several chickens, and a couple of cats who feast on unfortunate mice. At the base of the hill on the north side of the convent is the house of devotion, a small chapel where we gather seven times a day and once at midnight for the Divine Office, or reciting of prayers. I call it a house of devotion because those who enter it seem to want to be there most of the time, unlike my previous experiences at morning mass with Roughskin.

On the west side is the dormitory, which is divided into three sections. On the north end is the common dormitory, where the nuns sleep, and next to this is the Novitiate where the novices sleep and are trained so that one day they might become nuns. The guest quarters are next, where Adeliza, Mary, and I live while we wait for the arrival of the child.

The convent is poor but boasts one large icon: a marble statue of the crucified Jesus Christ which sits in the chapel's nave. Adeliza tells me he is nailed to a cross for claiming to be the son of God. He is crowned with a cruel wreath of sharp thorns which have been crushed into his skull. The statue captures the agony of his last few breaths. He hangs on the cross, capable of leaving it, yet remaining to die for me, Adeliza says. Well—not for me alone, but for all people, for all of our sins. I understand sin now—it is the evil within us taking action or inaction. It is a man stealing, a woman lying, a child hitting. It is a man refusing to provide, a woman unwilling to love, a child not obeying. This is what this Christ, this Jesus died for.

This is also the Christ whose birth we are to celebrate in just a short while. Adeliza has told me he came for this, to die. I remember the chapel where I gathered with Roughskin and the other servants for morning mass. That chapel was so filled with adornment that I would look from one icon to another, even at the few relics gathered from where Christ himself was said to have walked while he lived on earth. The chapel seemed cluttered to me, and though I understood the priest's droning Latin, there seemed no message for me in his monotone song. I spent the time thinking through other things, trying to stay awake. I kept wondering why so many of the icons were considered significant. As I stare at the dying Christ, the focus of their entire religion, I cannot imagine why they would need anything else to look at. This one statue seems to tell everything. His face is pained, his eyes searching for something. They are full of love, full of hope, full of things I cannot name.

I do not know a great deal about Mary, save she is Adeliza's closest sister and that she refused Bluebeard, though he had pursued her first. She has a knowing way about her—she senses things before they happen. I'm told she spent Adeliza's wedding night in tears, confident that the entire affair was destined to bring her family to ruin. I feel I catch glimpses of this when she stares off into the vacant air, as though concentrating on some solid substance my eyes cannot see. I wonder about her and the whole of why she has come to be with Adeliza. As we return to the convent, I smile at Adeliza who has walked off to cut some holly berry branches for decoration. I ask Mary if she is quite well, and she turns to me with an impish smile on her face.

"I am quite well enough for all that is to come."

I know not what to make of that, so I lapse into silence, wondering if I have become too familiar with her and overstepped my station.

"Rapunzel, you are so full of worries and doubts; don't you know that there is a life to be lived? You take on burdens that are not your own and then make them your own. I know what you are thinking."

This seems odd and rather arrogant, since I myself do not know what to think.

She smiles and continues, "Adeliza will be fine and able to leave this life behind her. She, of course, will probably never marry again, but there is a chance that one day she may meet a man she can trust. If not, she will not want for anything and will live in peace at my father's hearth. Is not that enough?"

"Of course."

"But it is not enough for you, is it?"

"Pardon?"

"You will not return with us to my father's home after the child is born, will you?"

I make no sound—how can I answer a question I don't understand?

"Where you are going you will go without us . . ." her eyes drift once more, and I walk away from her with slow steps to find something to keep my hands and my mind busy.

◌◌◌

IT IS past midnight and we have already said Matins in the chapel, but I cannot settle down. Though I don't know why, I find the past very near me. Is it sitting on my chest? Though I am lying unmolested in my bed, I cannot seem to breathe. I try to understand why my thoughts must always return to places I'd rather not revisit, but I cannot will them to do otherwise. The thoughts become a string of visions weaving throughout my mind, tying me up. They begin with the witch's smile as she told me stories, flowing to her screams as she chopped off my hair. I see her anchoring the braid to entice my beloved into the tower only to push him out. I can almost hear the sound of his cries as he falls and falls. Then I see the troubadour. What has he to do with any of this? He smiles, but his smile falters . . . he haunts me. What might have happened had I not left his company? Would he have known me, would I have allowed him to come closer and—what? I cannot fathom what more could have happened between us. I see before my eyes images of the story the players performed for me, and then the troubadour scowls before turning his back, saying, "It is too much for you."

The thoughts I had meant to sort through are now intertwined. I cannot understand their relationship to one another. I cannot unravel it anymore, but I know they are more real than I have ever been. I know the lies I believed before were wrong. I was not safe in my tower, but neither am I safe in this muted place.

The head nun is called the abbess, and when she finds me in the chapel alone late tonight, she comes over to me with noiseless steps, placing a rough blanket around my shoulders.

"My child, what troubles you so?"

I stare at this woman who has shut herself off from the world. Her eyes are a bright blue, reminding one of a cerulean sky in the summer. Though I know her to be past childbearing, she is still stunning, having lost but a few teeth at her age. All of the wrinkles in her face are kind, showing years of smiling and pondering. What has her life been? When did her family bring her here? Would she have liked to have married and had children of her own? As she sits next to me on the hard bench, I gaze at the coarse brown material of her habit, another reminder of her commitment. She gazes up at the icon I have been looking at, her eyes full of compassion, full of assurance. Peace is hers.

"I have not been brought up in the Church." It was not what I was intending to say, but I wish to be honest.

Her smile is kind as she turns to me, "I know, my child. You know almost none of our customs. Where were you brought up?"

"Far away from the world of men."

"You were cloistered until now? But not in an abbey?"

"Yes." If I were to tell her my guardian was a witch, how would she react? Would her concern dry up? Would she cry out for my burning, or would she tell me that there might still be a place for me with God?

"And your mother?"

"I was brought up by a woman who hates God, hates the Church. She hates everyone . . ." I shrug my shoulders. What else can I say to this gentle woman? I hope she has never encountered such hatred.

"Did she hate you?"

I never thought of this before. "I don't know—she always said she loved me, but her love was . . . difficult to bear."

"Rapunzel, I will ask our Lord to show you the way. He has something special for your life."

"Does he?"

"Yes." She reminds me of a child with a beautiful secret. "You must wait on him, and ask him to show you the plans he has for your life."

I feel myself squirm. Why must everyone have their own plans for my life? Am I to never to be in harmony with others, but always prodded and pulled to do their bidding?

A sudden knocking is heard on the chapel's door, and we jump in surprise.

"It seems we are not the only ones who cannot sleep this eve." She moves forward, her movements full of grace, approaching the door in her own time.

As she opens the door, a gust of wind and swirl of snow blow across the stone floor. At first, we see nothing; our few candles quiver, one blows out. Against the black of the night, it grows dark. A body falls forward onto the floor as a moan breaks the eerie silence.

"Help me, Rapunzel!" is the abbess's urgent cry.

I hurry forward to help pull in the body and shut the door. With much difficulty, we manage to turn the individual over, revealing a wounded young man, some seven or eight years older than myself, perhaps.

"Rapunzel, go and wake Sister Agnes—we must see what ails this young man and what can be done for him. Bring plenty of water and clean cloths. Hurry now, child." Though her voice steadies, I hear her earnest command, so I rush to do her bidding.

Sister Agnes is nearly silent, as always. Her dark skin matches the brown robe she puts over her cotehardie. It is the first time I have seen her black, frizzy hair uncovered, and I think what a mercy it is that we can both cover our heads most of the time.

When I return to the chapel with a basin of water and towels, I see the women are at work clearing the wound. At some point, the poor man was impaled with a sharp object, and it took quite a bit of candlelight to make certain the wound was free of all foreign objects.

This being done, they work at cauterizing the wound, a

heated piece of iron burning the flesh to stop the flow of blood and speed the healing process. The sharp smell of iron and seared flesh nearly makes me gag, but I take deep breaths to calm myself. After this, we move the poor man to the infirmary where we will continue to care for him.

⚓

THE PAST DAYS have been an exhausting blur. Mary and I helped Sister Agnes take turns with the young man as he drifted in and out of consciousness. We did not allow Adeliza anywhere near the poor soul, in case he developed some further malady. She seems satisfied praying for him in the chapel with the other sisters.

⚓

I FIND Adeliza sitting in the refectory as she is twining holly berry branches with ivy into a garland for decoration, something I wonder if she has ever done before. Her fingers, adept at embroidering, seem quick at the craft, and the room is filled with subtle smells I have never encountered before. She gives a light turn to me as I enter, and she smiles, holding up some white berries and putting them down with a sigh. "I suppose I will have no need for mistletoe this year—though you and Mary might if you were not stuck in this dreary place because of me."

"Mistletoe?"

"Why yes, I found a bunch while we were out the other morning growing on an oak tree, but I needn't have made Mary pick it. Seems inappropriate here." She smiles with a blush lighting her face. "I wouldn't want a priest to feel inclined to kiss me at Mass and break a sovereign vow."

I must look bewildered because she laughs at my ignorant expression.

"Don't you know that if two chance to meet beneath mistletoe they must kiss? Haven't you ever been caught, Rapunzel?"

"Not by mistletoe."

"That is a shame; it is quite an exhilarating experience —" A shadow hovers and touches her happiness. "—One that I suppose I am done with, now that I am a widow."

I ache for her loneliness. There is nothing I can do to relieve her of the pain she feels.

"It's fine; I know that I chose the wrong man. My life is not a ruin, nor is it what I once dreamed it would be. Still, I am alive and well." She lifts herself to her feet and balances by shifting with her new fullness before moving about the room.

"The sisters must truly love me to allow me to decorate as I please for the Christ Mass."

I glance around at the white-washed walls and plain, plank-board tables and benches. "They do not believe in decorating much, do they?"

"No, I'd say not." Her eyes roam the sparse room. "And, after my fortress, I find it comforting . . ."

"But now?"

"Well, it is time to celebrate, and we must have color for that! Come; help me find a way to attach this garland to the walls."

THE PATIENT

The young man's fever drops and rises with the coming and going of the day. He has been placed in a small cell of a room on a modest cot much like all our pallets, covered with a coarse blanket. The room is just big enough for his bed, and each of us takes turns sitting on a small stool beside him. Today he has begun uttering things in a language I am not familiar with. Mary was called to sit with him and began talking back to his dreams. I have caught a few words that I guess at in his babblings; perhaps it is related to Latin? She murmurs in a low voice, and with gentle hands she wipes his brow, her dark eyes softening as she comforts.

When I come in to sit beside him this afternoon, I stop outside the door, hushed, noticing her wistful smile at the young man. His eyes are open, but not clear, he still seems somewhat delirious. He speaks words of . . . I can't quite understand—love? He is speaking to her as though she is his love, and she speaks back in kind. I don't know every word, but I know this much.

It sounds like beautiful mush to me, having caught only *I have lost you, I know you,* and *I love you,* amid other words that I don't understand. I feel as though I am gazing on one of my books, one whose language I haven't mastered yet. All at once, I come to myself: this is no book, but a private moment I am watching, and I clear my throat. Mary's face turns to me, but her eyes take a moment to linger on the patient's face. "Rapunzel? Let me introduce Señor Dominico. He has come to meet Father Iohannes who will lead us in the Christ Mass, but he ran into trouble along the way." I note that she is speaking in *clerical* Latin, which I understand better in reading than in speech, but I adapt and follow her.

"You are a monk, then?" I assume, before remembering his full head of black hair.

"No—Father Iohannes is my father's brother. He has traveled far from our home in Catalonia in the Eastern Ports. I have come to tell him that my father is requesting him to return home before he dies."

"I am sorry to hear that your father is unwell." I look at Mary in confusion; this was not what they were speaking of before. This man is lucid; neither he nor Mary seem intimate with one another, but only moments ago he was speaking of having lost his love . . . of having lost her.

A smirk gathers around the edges of Dominico's mouth. "My father is not unwell; my father is manipulating his brother to fetch him home where he can begin working among the people there. My father considers himself a bit like a cardinal or the Holy Father himself; he knows best how everyone should serve God."

I cannot take my eyes from the man. He speaks as one who feels well, but his face—skin that should be olive-colored is blanched, dark hair curling with perspiration as he fights off another fever. Though he smiles, I see him shift; his eyes glaze over, and he begins murmuring in that beautiful, fragrant language that I can't quite catch.

Mary bends low and wipes his forehead. Shocking me, his hand shoots up, and he chokes on sad words that bring tears to my eyes as he pleads with her, touching her face. First he is gentle, then insistent, trying to pull her down to him. But she is tender as she takes his hands and begins humming in her sweet way. I've heard the tune before, but I cannot recall the words. It relaxes the patient, and he lowers his hands, allowing her to settle him back into the bed. After a while, he shuts his eyes and begins to sleep in peace.

Mary makes eye contact with me, and we step into the corridor outside the room. "He thinks I am his dead love come back. His moments of delirium fade without warning, though, and in those moments he realizes I am just nursing him; he knows who he is and what he is about. Then, he begins dreaming again, but he is awake while dreaming and looking at me . . ."

I close the outside door behind, once I have watched her walk out the door across the dirt yard with careful, measured steps, her burgundy gown sweeping the frozen earth on her way.

⌒⊱⊰⌒

Two weeks have passed since Dominico first came. Adeliza approaches me as we break fast together. The entire convent is fasting from meat and dairy in observance of the Advent. The sisters already fast from the morning meal, and some are fasting from the midday meal while they pray for delivery of the young man from his illness. I look up at Adeliza, happy that feasting will begin for the Christ Mass so that her rounding figure will have better substance than this dry bread and old porridge.

"Rapunzel, is Mary quite well? She seems so—" Adeliza's dark eyes drift over the small room, her hands resting on the uneven, rough planks that serve as a table. "—distant."

"Have you seen the young man?" I say after choking another swallow of the porridge. Perhaps I should offer to help make food while the sisters are hard at work fasting.

"No, the abbess asked me—"

"Yes, I know," I flash a mischievous smile, "but neither of us follows all we are told to do."

"I know . . ." A cloud crosses her features, and I frown, realizing too late where such a thought has taken her. "But this time I have obeyed, for the sake of my child." She pats her growing belly, an absentminded gesture; the fact that it is visible at all on her tiny frame is proof that she is halfway to having her child.

"Rapunzel, please—check on Mary for me. I am concerned about her."

Since being free of her husband and her obsession with his castle, Adeliza has been a sweet, excited little woman. She seems to enjoy the time she spends in the chapel or working. She often hums and sings, and I have noticed that the longer she is here, the more she engages in working alongside the sisters, whether in prayer or domestic chores. Of course, to the sisters' credit, they will not let her over-strain herself, and they still allow her indulgences, like decorating the dreary place with the holly and the ivy. She walks around with rosy cheeks, her belly before her, and a smile on her lips.

Now, though, her eyes are downcast. It worries me to see her distressed. "Of course, Adeliza, I will see what I can do."

"I know you will, Rapunzel. In truth, God has his hand on you, always using you to help my family."

I know not what to say to this, so I excuse myself to go relieve Mary from the patient.

I open the outside door without noise, since the wind is not blowing as it sometimes does. I hear them speaking in familiar tones once more, and as I open the door to his room I see Mary perched on his bedside. Dominico pulls her to him once more—and this time she allows him to kiss her.

I cannot contain a gasp, but Mary pulls away in haste and turns, almost running into me as she leaves the room. She is outside and halfway to the dormitory before I have the courage too late to call her name. I turn to face the man on the invalid's bed.

"I see you are quite well."

"And I see you are quite surprised." His words are heavy with his accent, his tone low and husky.

"Should I not be? Have you come to a convent to seduce a young maid?"

"Mary is not a nun, nor even a novice."

"She thought you dreamed her to be your lost love."

"I did, at first, but now I see she is my Maria." He pauses for a moment. "I have asked her to return with my uncle and myself to the Eastern Ports."

"For what purpose?"

"To wed, before my father."

"Did she say yes?" is my incredulous question.

"You saw her answer." He does not conceal his triumph.

"You don't know her, you don't know her people. How can you think to marry her?"

"I know much about her father; do not pretend to think I am ignorant of who he is. Of course, we would travel first to see him and obtain his blessing."

"But she cannot leave Adeliza until the baby comes."

"I can wait until Adeliza is ready to travel. I have much work to complete in the Northlands before I can return to my home. It was business and seeing my uncle that brought me here. Otherwise, I usually travel by ship to Trisse."

My head swirls with the implications of all he has said. Mary will leave her father's home for a land she has never seen with a man she has never known before two weeks ago. A man she might not have met if he had not—

"How came you by your wound, sir?"

"Painfully." He laughs and then coughs for a while.

"If you are such a wealthy man, where is your entourage? Your carriage, your men-at-arms?"

"I rode ahead, but they will be here tonight. You will see, little one."

"And your horse?"

"Worthless beast ran off while the thieves beat me." He looks at me. "You serve your mistress well, but I am the man I say I am."

"And Mary?"

"She is the woman I have been looking for."

⊂⊙⊃

HIS ENTOURAGE COMES as he said they would, arriving just before the abbot, Father Iohannes. The convent has never seen such a gathering, I think, but the men double-bed where they must and Dominico's servants sleep in the well-built stables with plenty of firewood.

Now that everyone is reunited and fed, the abbot calls us together. It seems that he has a test for his young nephew—or rather, it seems that the abbot has a test for his nephew and his betrothed to verify that their union will be blessed.

The abbot, who does not come from a poor monastery, stands in his robes, long white satin garments embroidered with gold thread, the design of a cross repeated again and again. Like all priests and monks, the top of his head is shaved in honor of God, and though the man must be in his fifth decade, his black hair stands out dark from his exposed scalp, no grey to be seen in it. He speaks little but uses his eloquent hands to express his thoughts. He seems to be one used to silence, more comfortable with gestures than with words, but when he does speak, everyone around him is compelled to listen and obey.

Having crossed himself, he asks that Dominico and Mary stand before him. As the couple moves to do so, I notice that Dominico still trembles a bit. "You are betrothed?"

"Once the engagement has been blessed by you as a representative of the Church, and then by Maria's father, we will marry."

"And what are you willing to do for your betrothed?"

"I will provide handsomely for her. She will have land and riches—the best of all I have will be hers."

"And you, dear lady, what will you do for your betrothed?"

"I will be a good and faithful wife. I will give him children as best I can."

"What do you desire of your wife?" The abbot's direct gaze does not waver as he watches Dominico.

"That she stays by my side."

"And you, puella, what do you wish of your husband?"

"That he loves me."

"But what of his riches?"

"I have seen what riches can bring to a marriage if there is no respect, no honor. I want his love, and in return, I will give him all of me."

"And you, sir, what of her beauty?"

"I do not deny she is beautiful, but I had beauty before and lost her. I only want Maria to be mine."

The abbot gives a thoughtful nod. "This and more shall be yours if for one month's time you leave one another. I require that you see none of each other after the Christ's Mass until one month's time has passed, and then we shall see what you desire of one another. That will determine if you are to be blessed before the Lord."

I feel a frown on my face, but the couple seems satisfied, as though relieved. I wonder what it is they thought the abbot would require of them.

THE TEST

All is darkness around me. I hear Paul's voice keening in the wilderness, shut off from me forever. "Rapunzel!" he cries, his voice an agony to hear, so I wade through the thick, heavy blackness, certain that if I try, I will find him. "Rapunzel, I cannot see you. She has taken you from me. Rapunzel!"

My legs are weighted down with the sludge of darkness. I am still struggling when his voice stops. I try to speak, but my voice is garbled and comes out in a harsh scream, raking the air senselessly. I form the words with my lips and concentrate; she will not stop me this time. "Mmmar lliiniiiiiiniii, owwooooww." I feel hot tears burn down my face in frustration. I will say what I must—I will! "Mmmmyyyyy loovvuuuu." Can no one help me find him? Can no one help me speak with more clarity? "Myyy loffff."

"Rapunzel?" His voice lowers, full of uncertainty.

I swallow—he understands, I will find him! "My loffff!"

Louder now he yells, "Rapunzel, I am here. Find me, I am here!"

The darkness still binds me, trying to hold my legs from moving, but I inch forward, now using my upper body and dragging my legs out of sheer willpower. I will find him!

"Rapunzel, I am here. Please, find me! Release me!"

My throat is freed, but now my arms are going numb and I fear I will fall forward, paralyzed. "Where are you? Where are you?" My voice begins echoing, distorting, and I lose all sense of where I am going in this black night. I need him to speak again to orient myself so that I can move towards him once more. But when he does, his voice comes from all around and I cannot understand his words. I begin crying, harder this time, for the noise assaults my ears; the darkness shackles me. I am reduced to nothingness, as I cannot move forward and am lost without hope.

"Rapunzel!" Adeliza is holding my shoulders, hunched down beside me, her candle lit on the nightstand beside me, shadows dancing over her worried features.

"Rapunzel, wake up!"

I begin to cry harder. A dam has broken within me, and my desolation engulfs me. "He is gone," I cry, "He is gone."

Adeliza takes care as she picks herself up and lifts me to a sitting position on my bed where she puts her arms around me and rocks back and forth, singing in a low voice.

I don't know how long I cry, but she never tells me to stop, simply lets me cry myself dry, ending with hiccups and burning eyes.

Sleep tonight, my love, sleep tonight
Sleeping tight, my love, sleeping tight
Let your worries run wide

Let me stay by your side
Sleep tonight, my love, sleeping tight.

Am I forcing something that is not natural? Why can I not let him go? Why do I still long for him though there is no hope of our reuniting? Adeliza rubs gentle circles on my back. She asks no questions and, after a time, helps me to lie back down. She smiles in a mother-like way before returning to her bed. I am grateful that Mary heard nothing, as her snores never change their snorting rhythm from her bed.

◌₂₉◌

THE NEXT MORNING I smile at Adeliza over our meal and whisper, "Thank you."

Her chin lowers. "You have done more for me, my friend. Please tell me, when you wish, if you are well."

I smile and nod again. How good it will be to share my burden. But not now—today is not the day to share such trials. Today we celebrate the Christ Mass.

I follow the nuns outside the walls of the convent and we begin decorating nearby evergreens with dried apples, thanking the Lord for his mercies. We tramp back inside to the kitchen and begin preparing the evening's meal, which will include only those items allowed during our Advent fast. But I have seen the two beautiful geese the abbot has brought, as well as a deer, and I know that our meals until Epiphany will be grand.

"Rapunzel—" The abbess has a suspicious twinkle in her eyes. "—I have an important task for you. We must make as many little oblong mince pies as we can. They represent Christ's crib, and it is important that we eat one each of the twelve days of Christmas."

I take time to think through how many I will need to make—and I am astonished! But when I look around at many of the sisters hard at work baking and cooking, I know that I am not alone.

This is a merry time as the eager women anticipate breaking their fast. I enjoy the note of excitement in their voices.

By evening we are exhausted through and through, but we are satisfied knowing that our meals for the next few days are ready. I smile at my stack of yummy cribs. I hope they taste as good as they look.

After baking and cooking all day with a wide variety of ingredients, it is difficult to imagine eating one last limited meal, but it is much more festive than it first appears. We enjoy tart cooked apples, sweet roasted Provence figs with laurel leaves, delicate white herring, strained peas that pop when I bite into them, cooked mellow carrots, salted eel, and many other fish dishes. I thought I would never want to eat another fish after all I had consumed during Advent, but I find that I quite enjoy this meal, concluding the fast on a happy note.

I look across our table of women to see Mary. The men have already eaten, as the room isn't big enough for both groups to sup at once. As we came in, I observed a longing look between her and Dominico. Tomorrow's mass will separate Mary and her betrothed for a month's time; I wonder how they will handle themselves. It seems I am not the only one thinking on this, for after the meal, as we return to our chamber to rest before the midnight Mass,

Adeliza sidles up next to Mary. "You will miss him a great deal, won't you, sister?"

"I suppose I shall." She sounds as though she is determined to seem unaffected.

"And what shall you miss the most?"

Mary looks puzzled as I open the door and we all step in.

"Will you miss how he smiles, how he talks, how he——"

"I will miss him, sister, just him. I will miss that we cannot become better acquainted during this time, but I will wait for him."

Adeliza smiles as she lays herself down. I come over and prop her swollen feet on an added cushion. "Thank you, Rapunzel." She sighs for a moment. "How did you know you should marry him?"

I retreat to my own bed, ready to relax, but wondering if I should leave while the sisters sort out details I thought already discussed.

"He asked me—and the word 'yes' was out of my mouth before I could think. I'm not sure I can explain it. It felt like someone else was saying it, but I knew it was me. As the word was spoken, I could see us, together at his home in the Eastern Ports, sitting by a hearth with two children playing nearby. It must have been winter, for our clothing was lined in fur. My vision narrowed to his face. I saw him smile at me—and all at once I was back, here, at the convent, and he kissed me." Mary's dark eyelashes flutter as her cheeks bloom red. "I know I am to be his wife. I have seen it."

I wonder at such a gift, to be able to see some things, though perhaps not what you would choose to see. How does one discern what is best to do with such a gift? Is it a gift, or a self-fulfilling prophecy, followed blindly until it has come true? I think on such things, but I do not voice them, lest the ladies mistake my meaning and believe I disapprove. I don't know what I believe. I lay back to rest until it is time to go to Mass.

"And what do you see for our Rapunzel?" I can hear Adeliza giggle, but I keep my eyes closed.

"Adeliza, I do not search for visions, they come to me."

"So you have seen nothing for our friend?"

Mary says nothing for a time, but I hear her shifting on her bed. "What I have seen is nonsense."

I sit up and look to Mary. "What have you seen?"

Both sisters stare at me, startled.

Mary wets her lips and closes her eyes. "There is a tower pointing straight up, unattached to any building. It has no door and no stairs, just one window—and from it, a man falls and all grows dark. There is another man, singing, asking you to help, and you come to him—but your hands are bound and all grows dark again. There are two women, yowling, screeching, about to tear one another apart, and all grows dark once more." She opens her eyes and looks at me as though she can see inside my soul. "I don't know what it means, Rapunzel, but that is what I have seen. Mysteries, stories, riddles, spells." Her look grows inward, reflective. "It's as though from far away I hear someone singing, but I don't know the words."

Now I lower my face, more confused than before I asked. "Nor do I, but that is my life."

"Who was he, Rapunzel?" Adeliza rolls to her side while Mary remains seated on her bed.

"I had a love, but we were—he died. Now I just . . . look . . ."

". . . for him?" Adeliza wonders.

"Yes, in some ways I suppose I do look for him. I cannot quite convince myself he is gone from me forever."

"You still love him."

"I fear I will always love him."

"Why do you fear loving him?" Mary leans forward.

I try to sort through my emotions; is there a logical way to make something of it? "I cannot let go of him, but that leaves me with nothing."

Our room is filled with silence as no empty words of comfort are offered. Both girls nod at me and we lie down in quiet rest.

⚬

By noon the next day, I feel weary of Mass, for I have now attended all three. The second at dawn seemed to mumble and moan on forever and I stopped trying to follow the abbot's Latin and instead allowed my mind to stray. When Mary and Adeliza went to freshen up, I stepped away, needing to be outside the walls again. I found the evergreens we had decorated the day before and stood behind them, quieting my restless heart with a deep breath. I find that I no longer wish to be here—but I have promised to see Adeliza through her pregnancy.

Since leaving my tower I have never stayed anywhere as long as I have stayed here, and for some reason, it seems oppressive. What good is it to sit inside these walls and pray and clean when there are people outside the walls starving, fighting, killing, and hurting? I feel wrong doubting these religious people who have shared so much kindness with me, but I question their purpose in seclusion.

What am I searching for? I wonder. A place to belong, a people to call my own, to live with, love, and serve. If so, it cannot be here, for though I am intrigued and confused by their God, I am convinced that, though their love may be genuine, their impact is slight and renders them ineffective. The God-child, whose birth we are to celebrate, came out of seclusion from the splendor of heaven to love a weary and war-torn world. If I understand right, he lived in poverty that he might heal the sick and teach the confused. How can one emulate him and live a cloistered life?

I shake my head, nearly expecting to hear a hollow rattle inside. Too many questions, too little understanding.

◌⟨⟩◌

IN A CONVENT, one is not allowed to give extravagant gifts as is the custom of some during the twelve days of Christ Mass. However, Mary, Adeliza, and I exchange small gifts. For the two sisters I have written out verses of Homer, translated that they might enjoy reading them in the future. They have given me a beautiful new wimple while I wait for my hair to grow back and have promised to teach me how to style myself more fashionably once we return to their father's house by shaving my eyebrows and moving back my hairline. I still wonder if I will go with them, but Mary seems to have forgotten that she ever predicted I would not.

On the evening following the Christ's Mass, Mary tells us how she had given a love token to her betrothed, a crocheted armband, so that he might think of her while he is gone. He gave her a bent copper coin, almost cup-shaped in its bend, to remind her to be loyal during their test. I have watched her fingering the piece while her eyes focus on something just a bit ahead of her, unseen by the rest of us.

I wonder at this custom of exchange; should I have given some token of love to my beloved? Did he feel less sure of me because I did not? I push these useless thoughts from me; my beloved knew of my loyalty and my ignorance of such customs. He would not have thought the less of me for it.

BEING USEFUL

It does not suit me to be inside overlong, and so each day when Adeliza takes her midday nap, I walk out into the bitter cold to find some relief. I know from the looks on the faces of the nuns that they find the same sort of relief in visiting their chapel, in praying to their God. They find some release, some satisfaction in unburdening their soul in confession and penance. I walk out into the cold and let it envelop me.

The snow of the past months has come and gone in a brief thaw. Instead, the ground is frozen and covered by ugly grey and brown withered remains while the plants sleep the winter away. How blessed they are to not encounter this hideous season of death. They flame with the brilliant hues of autumn and fall asleep only to awaken to the wet, growing green of spring. I remain here, waiting for spring to return, imprisoned by this frozen land . . . waiting for a betrothal to be blessed, for a child to be born, for my decision to be made . . . Where will I go when spring comes? Perhaps it is just as well she not arrive anytime soon, for I know not what I will do when her season comes.

I muse a bit more, wishing for something of interest to do. The cleaning of the dwellings, the cooking and preparing for the babe all seem to weary me now. Though I know the tasks have a purpose, I do not anticipate anything—and, in truth, I long to leave. But I ask myself again, where would I go?

My restless eyes scan the horizon, dreaming what is beyond the hill that lies to the north of the convent, when I see a slight movement out of the corner of my eye. I turn my head and catch glimpse of a child, a small boy no older than six or seven years. He stands hooded, clothed in rags. His lips are tinged with blue, his pale face emphasized by his freckles, a wide smile aimed at me. He nods at me and waves.

I wave back, unsure of how I should respond. Poor thing, I long to warm him! I hesitate but a moment. "Come, child, in from the cold."

His eyebrows draw together. "Come where?" His speech has an odd accent, but I can understand him.

"Follow."

He follows close, right at my elbow, but stops at once when we reach the top of the hill and look down into the convent's outer walls. "This is where the holy women live."

"It is that."

"I cannot come in, I'm no holy woman."

"No, indeed not! But you'll be an icicle if you remain out here, so inside with you!" I try to laugh.

"No, I cannot—it would be wrong."

My sigh is heavy; I entreat him to wait for me. I run

inside and gather some warm blankets and tie them around foodstuffs. I come back out to find him staring at me, his thin, jolly face lit up with unasked questions. "What should I do with this?"

"Take it to your home. The holy women have sent it to help you through the winter."

He laughs then and turns to go.

"Wait, child, what is your name?"

"Johannes."

"Well, visit me again, Johannes. I'll be expecting you." As he turns to go, I feel my spirits lift. Perhaps there is something worthwhile I can do in this place.

⊱·⊰

THE CHILDREN ARRIVE, finding me on another midday walk. "Johannes!" I feel the smile stretch my lips, "And you've brought . . .?"

He steps forward with two children, one girl a bit older and another little boy, perhaps younger, so close are their ages I cannot tell them apart.

"I am Margreth, and this is Albertus," asserts the girl. She is quite striking with large light-blue eyes above hollow chapped cheeks. "Johannes brought us your blankets and food. Mother wanted us to come and thank you. She would have come herself, but she is taking care of the twins. They have the croup."

I have no idea what this means, but I take it to be some malady.

"Can I bring you children inside from this cold?"

Albertus, who seems a shadow next to the brightness of

his siblings, looks at me with large eyes like Margreth's. "We cannot go inside—"

"Nonsense." I turn my back and start walking to the convent. I hope their curiosity will urge them to follow, and after a while they do. I glance back to see Margreth take the lead, though Johannes and his brother seem reluctant to follow.

I notice that once we reach the foot of the hill and approach the wall, the trio halts.

"Are we truly allowed inside?" Margreth's confident voice wavers.

"I don't know why you wouldn't be."

"We are not holy and . . . we have nothing to offer."

"Nothing to offer?"

"My parents, we are poor. We have nothing to bring the sisters."

"The sisters are not asking for anything." I'm not sure where her little mind has taken her, but Margreth seems almost afraid. "Margreth, I gave the blankets and food because I wanted to—no one should be cold and hungry when others have plenty."

She narrows her eyes as she looks up at me. "Are you a holy woman?"

I find myself laughing, "No! No, I am just staying here as a maidservant while we are waiting for . . ." I see their little faces, earnest as they search mine. "I am a guest of this place, but I am also a servant. When I see a need, I seek to serve. That is why I helped you. Now, come inside."

Something in my words or tone induces them to trail behind me, and soon we are by the fire, drinking cider across from the abbess who knows already of my desire to help Johannes. Her broad smile lights her soft features as she encourages the children to warm themselves.

"Margreth, you are the oldest?" She nods. "And Johannes, are you next?"

"No, Albertus is next, then there was Georgius, but he died last winter."

"I am sorry. You must miss him."

"Yes, we all do. He was great fun, but Mother says now he will run and play with the children on the streets of heaven." I never envisioned the streets of heaven—I never really envisioned heaven at all. All at once I think of my beloved's face, laughing as he runs up and down a cobbled road of gold with children . . . I blink my eyes, somewhat dazed, but the beauty of the image sticks.

"So he shall."

My eyes linger on Albertus as Johannes speaks. The quiet lad may not speak a great deal, but his light eyes tell of the pain of their last winter.

"And were you born after Georgius?"

"Yes, and then there are the twins."

Margreth, left out of the conversation for too long, set down her drink, the clay cup making a dull thud on the plank table. "They have the croup."

"Oh, that can be serious. Does your mother need a poultice?"

"She would be most grateful."

"Perhaps I could send Sister Agnes and Rapunzel to come and help your mother."

The children look confused for the moment, but before they can object, Sister Agnes is in the infirmary, gathering items to make a poultice. I take along the food the sisters and I have prepared in hope of the children's return, and we begin our short journey to a rough bit of land a few miles north.

⋘⊙⋙

THE HOVEL IS PASTED TOGETHER with mud and smells like smoke and dung. The mother has not been well enough to clean for some time. That is my first chore after we send the exhausted woman to go and rest in the family bed that huddles against the south wall. As I clean, Sister Agnes begins cutting and then cooking a load of onions to place in a pocket of thick cloth. I am fascinated by the contrast in our skin pigments as I watch as her brown hands show me how to apply the poultice to the chests of the sick toddlers. This, along with the herbs she has ground up and dissolved in watered ale, should break up and draw the phlegm out of the small children.

The hovel has just one room, with the family bed tucked at the back of the house and the flue-less chimney built into the eastern wall. A crust of filth covers a simple table of coarse boards, and benches of the same are pushed against the western wall. There is a grimy communal basin of dark clay; I have to clean it first before I can scrub their six mugs, four bowls, and three knives. It seems they have nothing else outside of the large cauldron Sister Agnes is using. I promise myself to carry linens and clothes back to the convent to clean them if I can; It's the best I can do for now.

Now finished with these chores, I take over chopping onion after onion with a dull blade. I look over at Sister

Agnes's back with bleary eyes. "Is this normal?" I wipe my nose once more with my handkerchief and watch as the woman turns away from the cauldron to me.

"Oh, Rapunzel, you look so funny! You're red all over!"

I stare at her, baffled. Is this the same Sister Agnes who barely speaks, and even then only in a whisper? Her eyes are puffy and streaming water, but her normally closed mouth astounds me as now the full lips are open and laughing. "Well, thank you . . .?"

"Oh, I'm sorry, I shouldn't laugh, but you should see yourself—well, I'm sure I look the same!" She wipes her eyes, and though the change in her manner mystifies me, I find her laugh infectious. One of the twins stops wheezing for a moment and begins to hack with a horrible sound. Sister Agnes rushes to the toddler and picks him up, holding him lengthwise over her arm, belly down. He begins to spit up into a wooden bowl she has ready for this eventuality. She places the child back on the blankets on the fresh hay we piled up on the floor so that he is propped up with the poultice on his chest. "Good, it is loosening. I hope the other fares as well."

I look at the other twin, whose eyes are closed, her face a yellow-grey color, lips pale as she rasps in each breath. Her thin hair is slick with sweat, pale against her forehead. "Do you think she'll be well?"

"I hope so." The plain woman's grey eyes are serious once more, darting to check that the mother cannot hear. "Some recover, others do not. But," she smooths the girl's hair back, "we will pray and do all we can." She stands and walks back over to the cauldron to cook another dozen onions that I have just chopped. "Stay with them, Rapunzel, and hold them up over the bowl as you just saw me do if you hear them coughing."

"Of course," I murmur, and begin my vigil, watching for signs. Four times I pick up the small boy and try to help him rid his body of the phlegm. I begin to sing songs as he cries, whatever songs I can remember from my childhood. The melodies come back with ease, as it was one of the ways I entertained myself many nights in the tower.

As the afternoon stretches into the night and the family returns to eat, I begin to worry over the little girl. She has not begun the deep cough that her desperate body needs but instead strains for each breath. The father helps his children get their food, but I can feel the intensity of his gaze. He has brought back a rabbit, and after their meal is over, he returns outside to skin it. I breathe easier until his frail wife rises from her bed to stand near me gesturing to the twin daughter, her speech stopping and starting, slow from fatigue and thick with her accent. It sounds almost Northlander, but not quite.

"She not come awake since yesterday . . . won't take broth . . . fear I will lose her tonight." I know the silent tears that flood her face have little to do with the onions.

Sister Agnes seems uncomfortable with the woman's emotions. Her lips pinch together as she returns to the cauldron and tells the older children to prepare for bed; we will stay the night and watch over the little ones. Margreth, Albertus, and Johannes all comply without a word. Their wide eyes haunt me; they have already lost one brother.

I begin to sing again and then, near the third vigil, the little girl shakes with a violent illness. I hold her while her tiny body convulses, trying to rid itself of the putrid stuff. By now her brother is peaceful in sleep beside the hearth, having already rid his body of the illness. His fever broke earlier and Sister Agnes told me he only needed rest and good food to mend.

As I hold the little one, Sister Agnes looks on, now boiling water and soaking cloths to help her breathe. The retching continues for several minutes and I startle myself as I begin to pray aloud. "Dear God, see the suffering of this child—please, take it away!" She does not stop at once, but her body begins to relax, and within a quarter of an hour she has finished. She accepts cool water and falls into a deep sleep, her fever having broken. Her eyes haven't yet focused, but I know I will never forget her or her struggle. I wonder at the strange prayer that seemed to come of its own accord from my tongue.

When morning dawns, we are on our way, promising the danger is over and that we will visit within a day or so to check on them. I am more tired than I have ever been before. Even as a kitchen maid, the physical exhaustion could not compare to this. I glance sideways at Sister Agnes, perplexed by the amazing abilities she possesses and the secret humor she hides. Who is she? "How did you know what to do?"

"I am no apothecary."

"But—"

"A sister, now dead, took me as her apprentice and taught me all she knew of herbs and their healing powers. I learned a great deal from her, and from each new person I help I learn more."

"Have you helped a great many?"

"No, people in these parts are wary to come to us for help. They consider us . . ." her unlined face becomes a mask of frustration, "they consider us . . ."

"Holy?"

"Yes, but also untouchable. I knew at once that Dominico was a foreigner because he came inside. No one comes to our convent for help. I wish it were not so."

For the rest of our journey, we are quiet, keeping our own counsel. All I can think about is the Christ the sisters serve with such devotion. Would he not want the sisters helping others? Isn't that what they want?

❦

"SHE IS CHANGED SINCE THE ILLNESS." Sister Agnes and I have returned for the third time to make sure the family is getting on well, but the mother talks in a strained tone, staring at her recovering daughter in a hateful way.

"Why do you speak so?"

"She is strange now."

I look over at Sister Agnes to try to understand why the woman seems so unnerved. The sister seems baffled as well and gives her head a shake. I have decided that part of the reason the abbess has seen fit to send me on these errands is to make sure there is someone who can communicate with the family. As efficient as Sister Agnes may be, she is not one to feel the need to communicate much to others. I turn back to the brow-creased mother. "In what way is she changed?"

The good woman shakes her head and moans, making some sign with her hands. For a moment time hangs still and I envision my witch's face before me—only it is the witch I never knew, it is the child she once was. Hovering before me I see the perfect little face she must have had before my witch received the curse of the old woman that forever changed her life. I come back to reality and snatch the woman's hand mid-air before she completes making the evil sign. "Why do you do this thing?"

I cannot fully comprehend as her mother rants in her strange language, but I catch, "She is no longer my child. She has been bewitched or—or she has been changed! She is not my daughter!" She, in hysterics, begins to shriek. With rapid speech, she begins throwing things in the direction of the weak girl. I whisk the child out the door, and her other children who had elected to wait outside come to surround me.

I stare at them while they stare back at me. I hold the toddler in my arms and try to hush her cries. "What has happened to her?" Margreth breaks the silence as she closes the door behind her.

"I don't know. She seems convinced your sister is a—"

"No, not Mother, what is wrong with *her*?" She points at the child and refuses to speak her name.

I look at the little one's brothers and sisters; they seem quite happy to remain within hearing distance, but no closer. "She seems well enough to me."

"Last night I heard Mother say she was a changeling. Is that true?"

I pull the little girl tighter to my chest. "I don't know what that is. But she is your sister, the same little one that— that—" I stare in disbelief at the fear and horror that appears across their young features, "—that your God saved just a fortnight ago. Do you not remember how ill she was? How ill your brother was? He began to rally, but your sister did not, so I cried out and she began to get well."

"You cried out?"

"Yes, I prayed, and she began to get well."

"Mother says she is not the same any more." Albertus's voice is dark, suspicious.

"Is your brother not still tired from his illness?"

"Not like her," I hear the small girl whimper against me. The children head back into the home and I remain outside, wrapping tight my shawl around the bundle in my arms. I begin to sing as I did when she was ill and the girl's whimpering subsides.

In a short while Sister Agnes joins me outside, saying in short that the boy is well and we had best return to the convent, bringing the girl with us. I glance back to see the mother blocking the doorway with her arms crossing her chest.

The wind grips me in its icy hold as I begin making my way back. At first, speaking seems impossible, but I try nevertheless. "Sister, what is a changeling?"

"Some of the people from the Northland plains believe that creatures switch human children for their own offspring to strengthen their bloodlines."

"What creatures?"

Sister Agnes looks at me, "Trolls, goblins . . . the creatures are said to prefer infants, but sometimes after an illness, they switch the children."

"But this is nonsense. Does the Church hold with such superstitions?"

"We will observe the child and see what truth there is to be found."

I tighten my hug around the child, "Will she be harmed?"

"The Church would never harm a child, Rapunzel."

I adopt Sister Agnes's manner of walking, eyes straight forward, one foot in front of another, and try to stop thinking, try to stop worrying.

I STAY WITH THE CHILD, intermittently holding and reassuring her by singing songs. When the abbess and Sister Agnes approach, the child clings tightly around my neck as though she is frightened of them. "Shhh, it will be all right, little one." But as I look at their grim faces, I wonder—will all be right? Will everything work out for this pale creature?

"Rapunzel, can you bring the child to me?"

I nod and I pick her up to cross the rushes that cover the floor. The small lady reaches out a hand to the trembling child and speaks in soft tones. "Oh, you poor frightened thing! You are God's creation and you will be safe here. We will baptize you with a new name once the abbot returns. Until then, we shall call you little Mary." The small girl takes her head out of my neck for a brief moment to glance up at the abbess, but her shyness entreats her to hide once more.

My hands stroke the silken white hair. I know the woman has a reason, but I cannot understand the need to change the child's name. "Why should she lose everything that is familiar to her in one day? She has already lost her home and her family; will it not confuse her further to lose her name as well?"

"It is *because* she has lost everything that she must begin anew." The kind lady pauses and leans into me. "You see,

Rapunzel, few of us choose this life because we want to. We choose it because we have lost everything else." Her smile is sad. "But in losing everything, we have gained what is best: we have communion with God himself through his Son."

Her words stir and perplex me. I feel torn by them, unsure of what she means and what I should do. I understand loss, but what can be gained from loss? The paradox seems ludicrous, but appealing, for in it there is hope. But is it a hope that will satisfy or disappoint?

"Come, let us find a good place for this child of God. She will make a great playmate for Adeliza's little one, don't you think?" We settle her into our guest quarters, knowing that soon enough she will be moved into the Novitiate once she is baptized.

⚬

THE WIND IS BLOWING hard against the stones of our walls, making me long for my roaring fire. The witch was being truthful when she said I was never cold atop her tower. Still, despite the chill in the air, I prefer to be here, somewhat useful. I rise in the dark and stretch myself out, convincing my limbs that the day must begin before my mistress awakes. I dress and fetch water before I nudge awake little Mary, who snuggles into the nape of my neck. I carry her and her clothes into the kitchen. Making her warm before we begin our morning chores, I kiss the tip of her nose and she smiles at me. I wonder again if she will speak; at her age she should, but not a word has she uttered since coming to live with us.

"What shall we have this morning?" I smile down at her. She heads to the large cauldron containing the pottage from the past few days. "You think we should add something to the pottage to make it sweeter?"

She smiles in reply. I set about to kindle the fire and then core and slice a few apples I have gathered from the cellar. Sweet child, she sits on a stool on her knees while her small hands pat the table absently as I set about my work.

"You will miss her." Adeliza's voice startles me as she enters the room.

I take a breath. "Yes, I think you and Mary will as well."

"Yes, but I will do well to think of her playing with my little one."

We are silent for a moment watching little Mary run to find a few blocks we have shaped for her out of wood scraps. "I miss her brothers and sister. It was nice having them come and accept our help. I suppose they won't return."

"It isn't probable."

A thought occurs to me as I stir in the apples, "What if your child is a boy?"

"He will remain here until he is old enough not to need the care of a woman. After that, there is a monastery where the sisters will send him when he is old enough." She looks at me with sorrow-filled eyes. "I know that what I do is right, Rapunzel, but I will miss my child so. I wonder if Hannah ever regretted her choice."

"Who is Hannah?"

"Do you not know the story of barren Hannah?"

Adeliza has come to accept my ignorance with grace, no longer questioning it. She reaches to steady herself as she sits down on a stool. "Well, as I remember it, Hannah was married to a loving husband, but she was barren. Her husband married again, as men did at that time, and his second wife gave him many children but was hateful to Hannah.

"Every year the family would travel and pray and offer sacrifices. I suppose it was like Lent . . ." Her brows crease for a moment as she tries to make an ancient culture more clear for me, but I don't know what Lent is, either. "And every year Hannah would plead with God to give her the child she longed for. One year, she wept so hard a priest came and rebuked her for coming into the house of God in such a state; he thought she was drunk. She cried that she was not drunk—simply asking God to hear her. The priest, Eli, took pity upon her and told her to go in peace. He blessed her and asked God that her request might be fulfilled. A year later, she had a son, Samuel."

"What a beautiful story."

Adeliza's hands stroke her belly. "Yes, beautiful. She fulfilled her side of the bargain, too."

"What bargain?"

"When she begged God that last time to hear her, she promised she would give him the child."

"To be raised by the Church?"

"Yes, and when he was weaned, she brought him to the priest who had blessed her and left her son behind. Of course, she visited each year and brought him clothes. Perhaps I will visit my child, as well." Her eyes drift off.

"What became of Hannah's child?"

"He became a great prophet."

"What is a prophet?"

She looks at me as though I am peculiar again, but smiles. "A prophet is a messenger of God, someone who hears directly from him."

I finish readying breakfast in silence, watching Adeliza watch little Mary play.

⁂

AT THE END OF JANUARY, the abbot returned. He spoke to no one and instead let the two monks who travelled with him speak of his few needs. He took himself to the chapel and began his fast. The sisters, in their experience and wisdom, did not interrupt, but seemed aware of a need on a higher spiritual plane. I could feel the tension, but I was hard-pressed to understand what it meant. Many took a vow of silence and it cloaked us, muffling my voice so that I spoke aloud only on rare occasions in a thin whisper. Little Mary was no more quiet than usual, and it seemed her cheerfulness alone helped me through this somber time. What could it be that concerned this people in such a way that their thoughts could be in prayer form, pleading for deliverance from something they dare not name?

A few nights before Dominico was to arrive, a blizzard stormed us, blocking all entrances and exits to the convent. All but Adeliza and Mary took turns out with the animals in the stables. We each waded outside, bundled against the freezing wind, breaking our feet through the crusted snow and struggling with each step. We kept the fires blazing and the animals fed as best we could. I was happy to do my part and even offered to take extra turns, grateful to be away from the tense women and their uncomfortable silence. Though I didn't go near the larger animals the priest's convoy had brought, I was happy to help as I could for the hens, cats, and goats the nuns kept. But soon I was back among the women. The stress was a tangible thing, Adeliza always staring at Mary, who was now fasting, hoping her betrothed was inside somewhere, safe.

RETURN

The pounding on the refectory's door breaks up a rather sedate meal. A man stands melting in our midst, and Mary runs to him, throwing her arms around him. As he unwraps layers and layers of stiff, whitened clothes off himself, Dominico becomes visible underneath. Soon he is seated by the fire, his feet and hands defrosting in warm water as he tells us his tale. "On returning here, I stopped and supped at a small inn in a nearby town. A strange man came in—though one could scarce believe him to be a man, so overgrown was his hair and beard. His fingers were useless, as his nails were curled under, and his clothes were well in need of cleaning. His shoes seemed at least two sizes too big as he stumbled around in them. The innkeeper spoke to him as a vagabond, but I interceded. I said if his money was good, why shouldn't he be served?

"'Well, I don't know, don't like his stink to scare off others,' the rough old man spoke.

"'Let him share my room,' said I with a grin, 'My nose

is frost-bit and I can't smell a thing.' I don't know why I spoke up for the creature, but he seemed to need someone to, and I was obliged to do it.

"That night as the weather began screeching, the man shared with me who he was and how he came to be in such a state. As the second son of a poor peasant, he became a soldier. But now, with no war to fight and no longer needed by a lord with too many knights, he had begun traveling, looking for something he could be useful at. He found a lord with three daughters who employed him for the planting season through harvest. He fell in love with the youngest, and they hoped to wed once the harvest had come in, but her father had other plans. He told the young man that he was not to allow a razor to touch his head, nor to clip his nails. He was to go out into the nobleman's lands and find someone who would treat him with kindness. At the end of two years he should return to the lord and tell him the truth of his lands so that the lord might honor those who act nobly. Of course, having given such a service to this man, this creature would be allowed to wed his daughter, if she would still have him."

"And why wouldn't she?" Mary interrupts, surprising herself, I believe.

"Because, my life, the man looks a wild animal! No woman would want such a man for a husband. A noble young woman would make eyes at a peasant if she thought him good-looking, but have him return in such a state and she will already have wed the closest noble-born son." His bitter voice accuses.

"No—if she loves him, she will take him as he is, even if he never shaves again."

"And if he has nothing to give her?"

"She will give him herself, and then he will have her."

The hall is silent but for the crackling of the fire. "I braved the storm to hear you say just that." His eyes are wet, his voice thick, and he looks away from her face into the fire.

Sister Agnes replaces the cooling water, and Dominico seems to relax as he thaws and gazes at Mary.

"What are you holding in your hand, Maria?"

"The coin you gave me."

"And has it helped you love me more?"

"Nothing but God could help me do that, but I have cherished it while you were gone." Her look kisses him, and unshed tears shine in her eyes, as though they had been separated for years.

"I thank you."

"And what do you wish from this woman?" None of us heard the abbot approach, but I imagine he witnessed the entire scene up to this point.

"Only that she love me, faults and all, and leave me never."

"And what do you wish from this man?"

"Only that he loves me, and let me do whatever I can to make his way easier."

"Let it be done." The quiet man bows and returns to his chambers for much-needed rest.

As I watch him leave, I wonder what calamity this man's prayers spared them. The blizzard should have caught Dominico and kept him from returning on time, perhaps from returning at all. Is the abbot so powerful, or does he just know how to entreat God? What must it be like to hear from this God you cannot see, cannot touch? The man is possessed of strength of confidence, and I do not doubt he has heard from his God. I wonder what things they have said to one another.

I gaze on the happy couple. Their eyes are bright as they whisper while he holds her hands in his now-warm ones. Their heads lean together, intent on one another. Soon, he will gather supplies so that they can return to her father's lands, and then on to his own lands, once spring has no longer muddied the roads and Adeliza is well enough to leave her child.

Adeliza sits alone on a hard bench. She is subdued, almost desolate. She touches her abdomen, as though stroking the child who sleeps there.

⚬⚬⚬

WHEN I HEARD THE CRY, sleep fled and I tried to remember where I was. It was high-pitched but ended in a grunt and I could smell something—something I couldn't identify, something sweet-smelling. I fumbled around, searching for a way to make light in the dark. At last, I could see Adeliza, wet, dripping with sweat. Her face was white, and then bearing down, red and blotched the next moment. I knew I could not handle this, so I looked around, waking Mary and then running about to find Sister Agnes and the Abbess. When I concluded these tasks, I huddled nearby, helpless, alone. I knew the child was coming, and there was nothing I could do to slow this down.

⚬⚬⚬

IT IS FINISHED; the child has been born, baptized, and buried. The nuns are saying prayers, and we watch as the mother, pale as death, hovers to decide if she should follow her child or remain behind in this life. There seems to be no use in either life or death. What good would come from her death? But the nuns pray, swaying in their habits, for a child they cannot bring back. What good will come from her living and always mourning a child who perhaps should never have been conceived—but was that the child's fault? I saw him before he sank into the darkness, swollen lids closed forever. They barely sprinkled him with holy water, asking God for his forgiveness before he no longer breathed. At first, Adeliza was silent; I wondered if she knew what had occurred. She would not let her sister go once she became lucid. There seems no point to my staying. I suppose I'll run away again.

◦◦◦◦◦◦

THE DAYS DRONE by once more, and Mary and I take turns ministering to her sister. When she is past her bleeding she will be better, the nuns assure us. I am not easy to comfort. Neither do I fret. I do what needs doing and make sure that little Mary is occupied. She is my one comfort, and I will miss her. I can feel that I will leave soon, but for now I know that I am not to leave yet. I feel as though a Great Hand is holding me back, will not release me—and so I remain, devoted to making certain that Adeliza is well. My devotion, it seems, has its limits. Is this hypocrisy? I don't know.

The child Mary comes to me at the end of our midday

meal and beckons me with a crooked finger. I follow her out to the stables where I see what she sees. She points in excitement: there, next to the barn, is a crocus peeking out of the melting snow. Have I lost track of time? Is it to be spring already? I look around me, at the sky, the nearby trees; no, spring is not yet come, but this little plant reminds us that, soon, it will. Little Mary stops smiling while she watches me musing until her brows draw down, and I realize that I have disappointed her.

"Sweet girl, I am sorry. You are right, this is wonderful. The crocus shows us that soon spring will come." The blossom is a bright purple and she touches it with a tender fingertip. She has already learned how delicate the balance of life is. I take her face in my hands and look into her eyes, eyes that are the same grey as her mother's. Eyes that, I pray, are more discerning than her mother's. "I hope you will always see the beauty of life, that you will always look for it."

She gives her most solemn nod, responding to my tone more than my words. She surprises me as she wraps her arms around my neck, holding tight as she gives me a wet kiss on my cheek. "Wuv you, Punzel." A great, huge smile comes over her face like sunshine coming up over the hill at dawn.

I begin laughing. I don't quite know why, but I begin to laugh. She laughs with me, and soon we are playing in the bit of snow that is left, heedless of the cold until Mary comes to find me. Adeliza wants me to take her to the chapel.

⊂∋∋∞∽

WE STAND IN THE CHAPEL. Adeliza takes my hand with her very weak one. She stands pale in her black gown of mourning; she has told me she will soon don the habit of a novice. I know what she is going to say, but none of it makes any sense to my mind.

"He has gone to be with God the Father; he will be safe there and feel no pain."

I try to stop the words that climb up my throat.

"Rapunzel?" Her quiet voice seems so fragile and I try to shake away the thoughts that keep coming to me. "Rapunzel, what is the matter?"

"How can you—how can you lose your child and be content that it is God's will?"

I did not mean to make her cry, but silent tears course down her cheeks. I feel a horrid thing wriggling in my stomach, I feel I should turn away and be sick.

She holds my hand firm, her weakness paling in the light of her internal conviction. "Rapunzel, I don't know why our Father took him from me, I don't know what purpose it serves—but I know that my place is here now, and I am at peace."

I want to howl. I can see her pain, but I can also see her peace. It is not that I wish to take her peace from her, but I need to understand it. How can she be at peace in the midst of such misery? "But your child . . ."

She rises on tiptoe and wipes away the tears I did not know I was shedding, "My child is safe. I no longer have to worry for him. He is safe. God has him."

"How can you trust God . . . this God? This God who," I lower my voice and glance up at the one icon the poor abbey could afford, "killed his only Son?"

"He did not kill his Son . . ." but now she looks uncertain. How can she explain to me when I understand so little of her faith? "I didn't understand for a long time, but Christ died for us, because we could not make amends for our sin . . . He died, and lives again so that we can be reconciled to God, our Father." She smiles at last and I back away from her.

"You trust your child with a God who offered his only child as a sacrifice for our wrongdoings, for what we can never make right?"

"He loves us that much." She reaches her hand out to me, as though to guide me back, but I cannot take her hand, I cannot follow her. She drops her hand. "I pray you will believe one day."

AGAIN

*M*y feet have begun walking once more. This rhythm in my journey pulls me along. I can hear it and I must step forward.

I am leaving again
I am going again
Unknowing again
I am going again

Over and over these words repeat in my mind with each step. Where am I going? Why do I leave when I know no more than when I first started?

It seems a month since I have allowed myself to think, to consider the tragedy and joy that fell on the convent before I left. Adeliza has continued her preparations to take the holy vow. I still don't understand what it means except that she will trade her beautiful clothes and dealings with the world to live in a stifled, cloistered home. She will never travel again and will almost never hear of her family.

She will remain near the body of the child she lost, and perhaps little Mary will be a comfort to her. The sisters rejoiced in her choice, and though her family may feel sad at her loss, it is an honorable way to live, full of order and contemplation.

Mary has chosen to travel first to her father's house to tell him all the news and then to her new home where she will marry Dominico. I do not know what I believe about these happenings, only that it is an odd turn of events—and that I had best leave, which I would have done anyway. I can never stay too long, it seems. Something inside prods me on.

I think of Adeliza's new position as the March winds whip around my face. The road is inviting my feet to keep treading, keep moving. Will Adeliza's imprisonment be different from mine, since she has chosen her tower? I shake my head. I chose freedom, and freedom I have in abundance, it would seem. So much so that I cannot stop for fear of— But my mind will not dwell here, and like my feet, I progress forward.

A sound. For a moment it is muddied with the shriek of the wind and though I strain—a cat! I hear it mewing but I cannot make out its shape in the late afternoon. I stop still, not sure how to proceed. The wind is moving the sound around, and I wonder at the wisdom of coming out in such weather. Will my witch come to me in a gust? I hear thunder in the distance. I know that I should seek shelter before the dark clouds move closer and block out the rest of the light, but I hear the cat once more so I linger.

I sense rather than see a movement to my right, off in the bush, a reasonable distance from the road. I pursue it, telling myself that I can take shelter beneath the trees in the coming rain. The land is hard and frozen, as the warm spring rain has not had a chance to soften it yet. I wonder what it will look like by the end of this month. Perhaps I should have stayed at the convent until April to travel. Ridiculous, restless feet!

"Cat? Are you there? Cat?"

Ahead of me, the wind is shifting and I see the blur of a shadow moving. It is the cat. I bend down for a moment, observing the odious creature. Why should I wish to make its acquaintance at all? It seems I already have, for this is the same creature who betrayed my confidence to the witch.

I walk by it without a further glance; it does not deserve my attention.

"Rapunzel."

I will not look at it, even if it *can* speak.

"Rapunzel."

I continue, pretending I am mute and deaf.

It prances beside me. "Rapunzel, you must listen."

"I know who you are."

"Of course you do—I am your cat."

"No, you are the witch's cat," I remind the vixen.

"No, I am your cat, she made me—"

"You foolish thing! No one can force a cat to do anything she does not already desire. It is your fault that my beloved died and that I am forced to wander the earth without aim." I feel the dark sky coming closer; the breath of rain begins to exhale a fine mist.

"Follow me and I will show you where to shelter."

"I'll head to those trees, thank you." I begin to trot to a

clump of trees near the roadside, but the cat nips my ankle. It is not a sharp bite, but uncomfortable nevertheless. I do not appreciate her candor even as she warns me that lightning enjoys striking tall things like trees. I stare at her, tempted to retort that, though there were a great many lightning storms, my tower and the trees nearby were never hit. Then I realize that it might have had something to do with the witch. I shut my mouth and follow her, wondering what trap the little beast is leading me to. The rain gets heavier and soaks through each layer of my dress. Without mercy, it sticks to me as I stumble to keep pace with the feline.

As we take shelter in an abandoned barn, I look up into a threadbare thatched roof. Will I find a corner able to keep me dry? Cat saunters over to me and settles herself down on the hay-strewn floor. She cleans herself at length, and when she at last turns to look at me, I stare into her odd green eyes. She stares back without blinking, and I am reminded of a game that the players enjoyed: the first to look away would lose. Of course, neither cat nor I have had a drink between us of ale or anything finer, so this staring match might last a long time. She manages to stretch without losing my gaze, hind legs first, then her front paws. As she stares, she begins to clean herself—and I swear, she's smiling at me! Insidious little devil.

She gives a slow blink and yawns. "You win," she concedes, as though granting me a favor, and prepares to slumber as the rain falls.

I am tempted to wake her, to throw her, to give her a beating. I know, though, that it is useless. I find myself dozing as I stare at the creature and finally wake myself up enough to lay out all the wet things from my bag onto the hay-littered floor to dry. We are sheltering in one of the only dry stalls. The air has a slight smell of musty manure, but I can rest. I slump in the back corner of our stall and fall asleep, facing cat to keep her from sneaking up on me come morning.

◌჻◌

I DREAMT the dream again last night. I could almost see his face—that is to say, I couldn't see his face. Everything in the dream was muddled, was marred. It was as though my mind was clouded, shrouded, lost in shadows. I didn't know who he was; I didn't know who I was. My mouth, the one part of me that I could feel or see, was open in a voice-less scream, and then it snapped shut. There was just emptiness.

I awake, knowing nothing.

A hand reaches out to clamp my mouth shut and for a terrifying moment, I fear that Bluebeard has returned to kill me. But this hand, though huge, is calloused. It's not the hand of my former master's, but of a more earthy character—a thief. My belongings are snatched from their drying places, and I am shoved into the ground by two other swarthy characters speaking in a strange tongue. I cannot understand what they are saying, but once they have decided I have nothing of value, I am slapped and sent on my merry way, pushed out the barn door. Merry indeed—they have destroyed my wimple, which I have used to hide my hair, and ripped my surcoat with their pushing and shoving. I take the side-less garment off, making do with my two lower layers; my cotehardie and chemise seem fine as I brush them off. The surcoat won't be too difficult to mend, though where I will find needle and thread is beyond me. As I stumble away, blinking in the morning light, I decide not to worry about it now, just put distance between myself and the scoundrels.

I muse that I am fortunate they did not mishandle me further, though one of them looked discomposed once he saw the state of my hair. I am sure I looked quite ugly to them, quite undesirable. I suppose I had no further use after that. They never discovered the pocket sewn into my chemise where I secreted away my earnings, and since I was still wearing it when they found me, they never realized what they might have gained.

As I look around, I realize I have little idea where I am or where I am going. If it is morning, and if I can return to the road, I will travel towards the eastern sun—but I'm not sure where the road has gone, and I cannot remember which way I followed the cat when I chased after her last night.

Cat. I stop still in the middle of the now-soggy field, nothing near me but the empty, leaky barn and a few scattered scraggly trees that were once pushed back to make room for a crop. Cat—where did she go? I look for an elevated spot to sit down, wondering if the thieves allowed me to retain any of my food. Aha! I see they have left me a soggy heel of bread. What joy is mine? I eat it and think that I will not have to worry for drink since the bread has supplied that as well. Nasty mush!

"Where to now?" I don't even know who I am asking, don't know where I am going, not even sure what I am looking for . . . But a ripple of wind entices me. For no rational reason, I am encouraged and stand. I will continue my journey, such that it is.

⋘∞⋙

I'VE FOUND THE ROAD. I should say *a* road, for I am not certain that it is *the* road I was lately traveling. It seems I've lost my sense of direction since the night of the storm. Every morning for the last week, I have woken somewhat bewildered, almost too stupid to put two thoughts together and find my way back to the narrow, brown road, where I might come across something useful. I can't quite remember—was I traveling east? Or was it west? I suppose it doesn't matter, I don't know where I want to go anyway.

Though spring is coming, it is cool and the birds are only now beginning to return. Therefore, there are no eggs for me to gather. There is no food I can scavenge from the trees, though I have gathered several acorns and begun to chew on them. Amazing what will content a gnawing stomach for a short while. I did happen upon a rabbit and I killed it. I did not know I could do such a thing—it left me quite bloody and guilt-ridden. I have never stopped to worry about the animals I ate before now. Killing a thing makes its life more real, I find. But, as I say, I ate the small animal and wanted to pray or perform some such thing for my aching conscience and the sacrifice which appeased my throbbing stomach. At this point, I am just grateful to be back on the road, any road. I hope I might find someplace soon and use some of these coins to buy food I need not bloody myself to eat. It is disappointing to find I would pay someone to do what I loathe.

⚬

THIS ROAD IS PECULIAR. It seems to wander on and on. Once I have looked down it a ways, I often think I see something coming—but then I find the semblance of the image has evaporated and I am left wondering what it was that I thought I saw. I am half tempted to venture into the wood that lurks now at my right elbow. I am curious about it. I thought most of the trees had thinned and I would see no more until after encountering the next village. But suddenly one morning, they sprang up, thick and dark, full of webs and questions, and I feel my feet prompting me to tiptoe inside. I have been sleeping on the opposite bank, alert lest anyone should come by the road, but no one does. I have listened for footsteps tripping out of the trees, but they are not there. It is so quiet, and I have nothing left to eat, no more rabbits coming by, and all the acorns I gathered have emptied from my stomach. Though it is noon, I decide that I will halt my journeying by this aimless road and search for sustenance in the dark wood.

THE DARK WOOD

It is dark. I knew it would be dark, but after sitting across from the grove on the opposite bank and studying it in the midday sun, it is surprising to find oneself engulfed so wholly by darkness. I might even think myself in a different realm. The trees are tall, and their leaves—yes, to my surprise the trees are dressed as though it were summer—give such a thick canopy that one cannot tell the time of day or night once inside this haven. I shiver and wish I had a candle. I will hold still until my eyes can better see, and then I will continue.

There is a noise, a whispering that brushes through this wood—but it is no solitary voice. Instead, it sounds more like a mirage of voices smeared in several conversations, but there is not enough audibility to understand what is being said. It is a dark kind of murmuring, and I feel almost an ominous musical tone calling to me as I trip over roots and stagger around.

"Is anyone here?" My voice is pale. The voices stop,

and my feet stop as well, wondering what enchantment I have broken.

There is a slight stirring to my left, and my heart beats boldly as I strain to hear another sound. There is another murmur at my right, and then behind me a tone of ascension.

They mumble a question at me.

"Pardon? I cannot understand you . . ." My voice trails off, my mouth ajar with unasked questions.

"Child," a clear, sweet-sounding voice speaks, "why don't you come inside? You must be hungry."

I am still straining to see. "But—inside where?" I am blinded as soon as I utter the words by a bar of light hitting me as the darkness splits in two. A door encrusted with vines is pushed open by an unseen hand, the broken vines swinging and blocking my view from what lies ahead of me.

"Here my child, come inside."

A warm aroma of baked goods wafts out the door and tickles my nose. I follow my stomach inside, faltering in the new light. A gentle, age-worn hand firmly takes my arm, guiding me to a seat at a table where I am fed. Dizzy with hunger, I am having a difficult time focusing. I try to orient myself while I chew.

"Not so fast, you'll make yourself sick, my darling." The spotted, veined hand pats my arm, and I look up to study the face of the old woman. It is comprised of a patchwork of quilted wrinkles. Her eyes are two dark pebbles resting in the folds of her skin, and her toothless smile is kind. She pours a steaming cup of cider, and I can feel my body relaxing on the hard wooden bench as I dig into the trencher before me with dirty hands.

I should be asking questions, I should be more cautious, I should be noticing things. In truth, all I can think of is the roasted bird and vegetable pottage. I recall the cautions the sisters used to speak of when talking of the seven deadly sins. I suppose after so few meals I am giving into gluttony, but my mouth refuses to stop.

I slow down as I weary and begin to feel my head tip forward. Someone catches me, and I am being carried away. I don't know who carries me or even care where they will take me. My stomach is full and I allow the darkness and dreams to overtake my drifting mind.

⚜

"GOOD MORNING, MY WIFE." For a moment I believe my love is in bed with me, that we have escaped the witch as we had planned and we live together happily as man and wife. But my mind startles the rest of me awake as I do not recognize the male voice addressing me.

"What?" is the most intelligent thing to come out of my mouth as I try to rise. Someone has replaced my clothing with a night shift. I clutch the blankets tight to my chest and stare at the handsome stranger before me.

"Don't be frightened," he says, and leans forward in his eagerness.

"Step away!" I order, sounding shriller than I would like. Though he moves away, he grins as he does so. I lick my lips as I compose myself. "Now, who are you?"

"What do you mean, who am I?"

Grant me patience! "I mean, what is your name and what business do you have coming in here to my—" My what? What is this place? A quick glance says I am in a bedchamber of sorts, but whose? "—presence—uh—unannounced?"

"Pardon?"

He looks bewildered; perhaps *he* doesn't know who he is. "Do you have a name, sir?"

"Of course: Nicholas."

"And, Nicholas, why are you here, waking me up?"

"I'm your husband, and it is time to rise, my love."

I feel sure I will faint soon—*husband?* "What?"

He comes and kisses me on the forehead before sitting next to me on the bed. I try not to move away, but to listen. "Now we're back where we started. Matild, I love your games, but this morning is not the time; we have too much to do, and I need you to come and help with the babes. They are restless in their chairs and I am not much for feeding them by myself."

"The babes?"

"You were so tired, I let you sleep. I know they have been a handful with teething. Love, are you sure you are quite well? Come down and Cook will get you a bit of breakfast and you'll feel quite right again." He kisses me and helps me to my feet after placing slippers on my feet and wrapping me in a robe. His pattern of speech seems foreign to me, even outside of the fact that I have no idea who he is, where I am, or who he thinks I am.

As we walk through the door, my hand drops from his and he dematerializes, vanishes in a snap. I see instead the old lady from last night moving towards me from the front of her home.

"I thought I heard you up and moving. Did you sleep well?"

I realize stepping into the hall and walking into the light has changed me from a moment ago. I am no longer in a nightshift, but my dirty clothes. I put my hand to my head and feel my bristled, unkempt hair. "Yes, I think so. My dreams were . . ."

She reaches up to put a hand on my shoulder, "Oh, they are quite vivid in this wood, are they not? Especially in that room. I like to always put my guests in that room; I think it allows us to think through things."

"To think through things?" hums across my lips.

"Child, if any had things to think through, it would be you." Her smile is kind, and she once more pats my hand before she takes me to the main room where she finishes preparing a breakfast of fried fruit and bread while I dip myself into a large barrel full of warm water. After scrubbing my hair and every inch of my skin clean with an abrasive cut of soap, I feel refreshed. The fruit is tart and the heavy barley bread is toasted and glazed with sticky honey. I fill my belly with bite after bite, unable to stop myself from moaning in happiness.

The day is lovely, and I feel plump compared to the depleted Rapunzel who entered the evening before. The old woman, who tells me her name is Dorothea, fills the day with cooking and sewing and washing dishes, her voice filling the corners of the warmly lit house. She sits me down and shapes my mass of unruly curls with scissors and tells of visitor after visitor who has come to her wood and entered her house. She smiles and says she's glad that now I have come.

By evening I am exhausted once more, though this time I walk myself to the back of the house into my room, removing the new outer clothing she has given me. I lie down in my chemise on a bed of packed leaves that crunch as I move onto my side. When I shut my eyes, I hear something rustle, voices gathering in the dark. I cannot stay awake to contemplate further, so I float into another world.

NICHOLAS IS NEXT TO ME, sleeping; his pleasant breath in and out, his chest rising and falling regularly. I am calmed and dismayed by the sound. Part of me is comfortable, but another part of me feels wrong. I am in someone else's place, abusing the privacy of her bedchamber. In quiet, I rise and put my bare feet down on a thick rug. Unused to such finery, I stare in the moonlight at my pale feet on the rug and wonder at the pattern woven into it. I step soundlessly to the open window and stare out. I am not in a wood, but in a city of sorts, though not too close to my neighbor's house. I can see it from here—but no, it is a barn, hard at first to distinguish in just the light from the moon. I walk to a dressing table and stare at the porcelain basin and the beautiful pitcher beside it. The breeze is cool outside, though more like early summer than spring for the windows to be open and the water in the pitcher to be lukewarm instead of icy. In front of me, I see an image of a young woman my age, moving in sync with my movements. Her hair is long and dark, and there is something ghost-like about her, from another world. So intent am I on staring at her, I don't see the image coming up behind her until it places a hand on her exposed pearl-white shoulder. I start when I feel it and turn to Nicholas as he smiles down at me, who puts both hands now on my shoulders.

"Why aren't you sleeping, my love? Did the babes stir?"

My voice is stopped up and struggles to get out.

He peers through the darkness at my face.

"Who am I?" My whisper remains unacknowledged as he pulls me to himself.

"Come to bed, Matild." He leads me to bed and pulls me lengthwise into his chest and strokes my hair. I try to still myself, calm myself, tell myself it is only a dream from which I will sooner or later awake—and so why not enjoy it? But I feel panic rise as he begins to kiss me and speak her name.

"Don't hold yourself away from me, Matild. Are you sad? I will hold you all night. Have the dreams come again?" He seems so worried. I wish I could comfort him, but I long to run from this man who has lost his wife, run from this place and her image. I must be somewhere near —why can I not find myself?

I feel myself stiffen with resolve. I don't belong here.

"Matild?"

"No, I'm not Matild."

"Matild . . ."

"No, I'm not your wife. Please, I don't know how I came to be here—" My tongue seems useless.

"You would not be here if you did not wish to." His voice darkens. "You chose the room, and you have chosen to lie in my bed. Now, *Matild,* I will comfort you."

I spring out of the bed and rush toward the door, but at once he is already blocking it. With reason slipping away, I back towards the window.

"Come, Matild."

"I am not your Matild."

His laugh is a hideous, hard thing. "I know that, and I am not your *beloved Paul,* but we all have to make do somehow, right, Rapunzel?"

I need to breathe. My hands catch at the curtain behind me, leading to the cool space between window and sill as his form creeps, relishing my pungent fear.

"Now you say—well, whatever you wish to say. And I will pretend to be your fallen love, and you will pretend to be my lost Matild."

"I don't wish to pretend."

"Yes, of course you do." His voice carries a seed of doubt. "This is how we will survive. I will meet you here at night and—" The room is transformed, the very rug beneath my feet gives way and it is my love standing before me, whole, intact. "Rapunzel? Say you'll meet me here. This is the one place she cannot find us."

The window at my back is still there, but it overlooks the wall, and beyond it I hear his mare whinny. My chemise billows with the wind.

"But how?" My voice comes out small, too small for the question it holds.

"This is the only way." Paul's steps have covered the floor to me and he embraces me. I take in his earthy smell, his firm embrace. I fill my senses with him until I am swimming, gliding away. I awaken alone, with a curious indention on the bed beside me.

DREAMS

The days here are full of bustling and happy talking and so much joy that I can scarce think my own story through. I don't mind the days a bit, or the time-consuming tasks that have made me a better cook and baker. I love my time with Dorothea. We work together in the main room, rocking chairs pulled up next to one another before the hearth so we can sew and mend. The wood keeps the home sheltered and cool, so we have a low-burning fire all day and bank it before we go to bed at night.

We rise often from our sewing to complete other tasks. On the far side of the room rests an oak table, a place where we chop the vegetables and fruit Dorothea keeps stored under the trap door. I often stand chopping while Dorothea sits on one of the stools to pluck birds or skin the rabbits she has no qualms about killing. She does her killing outside, where I hear a short squawk or shriek. Each week we have fresh meat, and I feel stronger for it. Every day we scrub and dust and sweep, so the house is always clean. In the midst of all this activity are stories, each story binding us closer together. Dorothea and I are never at a loss for words. I tell her stories from the books I treasured from my tower, and she tells me more and more of the strange visitors she has cared for. All of them are enigmas, and I never know whether or not to honestly believe her. It reminds me in a small way of listening to my witch—but Dorothea's stories have no bitterness, always carrying some fantastic storyline that leads one back to trust in the God of heaven.

"Ay me, I do get tired. I remember, when I was young, how my dear old granny would speak of the aches in her hands, but she would smile and keep kneading bread or sewing. I thought one day I might grow old, but I never thought to have aches in my hands." Her eyes twinkle. "I suppose it's better than having no hands at all."

I look up from the quilt she has given me to piece. "No hands? Whoever heard of such a thing?"

"For a young woman with such great knowledge of books, you have learned very little about the woes in this land." Dorothea seems to understand innately that I am a stranger to the world and have little experience with people, but that I am keen to learn. Each of her stories seems bent on teaching me something, and as the stories keep my mind from thinking about the coming night, I give myself over to her teaching.

"The handless young woman who came to me had a horrible story, one she could not bear to tell me for weeks. She sat and wept every day, quietly, so as not to disturb her babe. But as time passed, she grew to weep less."

"How did she know how to find you?"

"All who are meant to find me do—but they don't realize they are looking for me, now, do they?" She stands up from her mending to stir the vegetable pottage over the fire. As she lifts the lid, the smell of onions, carrots, parsnips, potatoes, and leeks all cooked with barley sneaks under my nose, and I sigh in peace as she settles down once more to tell her tale.

"Her father, a poor miller, had been tricked by a wizard into exchanging whatever was behind his mill for great riches. At the moment of agreement, the miller thought only of the apple trees he would trade for riches. He did not suppose his daughter was there picking apples for his favorite meal. In three years' time, the wizard came to collect the girl—but she had washed herself pure and drawn a circle of chalk around her so he could not approach. Each night he returned to check on her and forbade her water, but she remained pure for the tears she shed, so he still could not approach. Then, missing the touch of her parents, she reached out for an instant—and the wizard's curse took her hands while they were outside the circle.

"Horrified, and knowing the wizard would soon return to capture their poor daughter, the miller and his wife strapped provisions to her back as quickly as possible and sent her away, hoping their handless daughter might elude the evil wizard. She managed to travel with the aid of heaven, her stumps miraculously healed over by her own tears . . . but she could not reach the food on her back. When she stumbled into the king's garden, famished and exhausted, she reached a pear with her mouth that was hanging down on a low branch. She only ate one, for she did not wish to deprive the owner of his food and had every intention of finding him, come morning, to make payment. But her weariness kept her from finding the owner come daytime, and she rose by night again and ate once more. This time, she was found out by the sleepless king who happened by, and in the moonlight her strange movements were first mistaken for that of a fairy. Once he recognized she was a young woman in a grave situation, the king had silver hands made for her—and soon they were wed."

Dorothea rises once more to punch down the bread that has been rising near the hearth and begins shaping it as its warm, yeasty scent permeates the room.

"And the wizard?"

Dorothea looks at me through her small eyes. "You are perceptive, Rapunzel. The wizard was not satisfied with her happy ending. No, he sought her for his own, and if he could not have her . . ."

"Did he kill the king?" I can't quite look the sweet woman in the face. I know she will see the rest of my story there if I do.

"No—he sought to confuse him, to twist their love into something ugly. When the king went out to war, as kings are like to do, his young bride had their first child, a beautiful son. The king's mother, who loved the young woman as her own, wrote to tell her son of his heir, but the wizard switched the letters while the messenger slept, and the king received a letter saying that the child was a changeling."

"A changeling?" This intrigues me, and I think of little Mary; I want to know if there are such beings.

"But the king had the good sense to do nothing rash

and wrote back that they should be well-cared for until he returned to see to matters. Not having achieved what he desired, the wizard continued to meddle, sending back a letter, seemingly from the king, demanding their death. When the good king's mother wrote back many times begging for mercy, she first received no reply, and then another brutal forgery came from the wizard. Fearing for the queen's life and that of her grandchild, the king's mother made them leave with the heir strapped to the queen's back.

"And one night, traveling through a wood . . ."

"She found you."

Dorothea smiles at me over her shoulder. "Yes, of course. The God of heaven led her here, and here she mended. Her son was a delight to us both, and though she did cry a bit more than I normally allow, she soon became well, and the wizard's spell was broken."

"How?"

"The horrible wizard died. When the king returned home and realized what had happened, he searched for her all throughout his kingdom, but until he humbled himself to ask the God of heaven for help, he had nothing. Then, one night after praying and crying—"

I raise my eyebrows. "Quite a bit of crying in this tale, Dorothea."

"Well, I tell it as it happened, and some are more tender-hearted than you and me," she winks. "After praying and crying, an angel led him to me, and I reunited him with his lost wife and child. And they lived happily, I am sure."

I stare at the bright pieces of cloth I am piecing

together into a star pattern. My hands stop moving as I think of all the troubled souls Dorothea has helped find their way. ". . . But all that time, all that time wasted apart."

At first she says nothing, but puts the bread in to bake. She brushes off her hands on her apron before taking it off. "Time in which you learn something is never a waste, Rapunzel. For a king to humble himself to pray for help is no simple thing. For a weeping woman to learn to be at peace, to relent from weeping, to stop running—no simple thing, either. I think they made a better marriage of it for all their trouble."

But I have little time to dwell long on her lessons; there is too much to do, and Dorothea begins speaking of *those* who are coming. She says it with such delight that I need not ask who is coming; I know it must be her children. They are coming back to see the dear old woman. I imagine I will have to sleep by the hearth while they are here, but I won't mind because they will bring her such happiness with their presence. For a moment I am reminded of another home in the wood when a family came—but Helga's family was under a terrible curse, and as the time for the visit came near, anyone near the house could feel the oppression. Not so here, just unending happiness.

AT NIGHT, he still comes to me. I wear myself out during the day trying not to think of him, reminding myself that tonight he might not. Then, all at once, there he is, in my sweet, beautiful tower. I am no longer shy and I wrap myself around him, uncaring of anything but his smiling face, his strong hands and his lips that speak on till morning, telling me new stories and adventures, full of where he's been and what has occurred. It is as if the night he fell never happened at all. My head is still heavy with my locks, and now there is no need to worry for the witch. He holds me all night, never needing to go and return home, he never leaves me any more. He just stays and stays, and I can feel him loving me—though by morning, of course, he is gone, and my long hair is shorn again.

But all is well. Of course it is. This is life, the one I love. I am split into day and night and, as long as I can, I will remain here, happy to be content.

My mind is rootless today. I am having a harder time than usual concentrating on the work at hand. I can feel my beloved close at hand—but when I close my eyes to savor the longing, instead I see Nicholas's face. I must keep my eyes open today; Dorothea will help me. As we work, Dorothea seems to notice my preoccupation. "You look rather worn, my dear. Have you not slept well?"

Dorothea's words wake me. I'm sure I have been performing duties all morning, unknowing what my hands are doing.

"Yes—I mean, no. The dreams, they . . . well, I think I have not been resting as I should." She looks so worried; I try to set her at ease. "Don't concern yourself, I will be fine." I finish drying the dish I realize is in my hand and put it away in her cupboard, then begin looking for another task for my hands.

"Child," her voice is soft, "at night, when you dream, are you sorting things?"

I find myself shaking my head, but I say, "Of course. I think through what you have told me, what we have spoken of and . . . I suppose I am overthinking the past."

"Oh, the past is full of many wonderful things, and it is easy to forget where we're heading."

"What do you mean?"

"When life turns us unexpectedly down a different path than the one we might have chosen for ourselves, we can find it difficult to focus on where we are going instead of where we would like to be." This is the most eloquently I have ever heard her speak. I listen with care as I begin scraping out the cauldron.

"Is that what I've been doing?"

"No more than anyone else might in your place. But, Rapunzel, you'll find it more profitable to place one foot in front of the other, to focus on doing what is right, focus on the life you now have and quit wishing for what you might have had."

My eyes smart and I bite down my retort. How can she know the pain and injustice of my life? How can she judge me for enjoying this little rest when I have so long traveled looking for something worthwhile? Is my life here in this quiet wood not meaningful? I give my head the smallest shake and pretend to be interested in the story I know she will use to try and teach me.

"Rapunzel, you are not the only mistreated young maiden. Once there was a girl, the youngest of eight children. She lived alone with her widowed father after the older children grew old enough to leave home. She longed to do something grand, but she could never seem to find her way. When her father remarried late in life, the poor woodcutter had little to offer his second wife, but she considered the young girl an adequate servant. The selfish woman had a vain daughter, and together they made the true daughter's life a misery. Each day after the woodcutter went about his work they set up difficult tasks, each worse than the one before, for the young girl to complete."

I sigh, knowing the girl's life will get worse before it gets better. I concentrate once more on my occupation, now scouring the cauldron.

"One day they asked for a hawk. It took the girl the better part of a week to find a hawk's nest, from which she took a young bird and brought it back to her stepmother and stepsister. Upon her return, the two had another difficult task ready: they wanted fashionable clothes like the ladies of court wear. They demanded the true daughter find silkworms and weave them two dresses each. This task took years for the young girl to complete, but she was determined. At long last she collected enough silkworms and made the dresses. Of course, the more tasks she completed, the greedier the other two became, and the more resolved they were to have whatever they wanted."

"What of her father?" I interrupt. "Why should no one protect this poor girl?"

"The man was weak-willed and allowed his second wife the leeway she craved to abuse his daughter."

"But he should have protected her."

"Yes, he should have, but often people do not do as they should, and the innocent suffer." She looks at me for a moment, stopping her cleaning, but soon her hands resume their scrubbing and her melodious voice picks up the words they laid down. "One day in the middle of winter, the stepdaughter had an awful craving for strawberries. The true daughter was sent out into the cold to locate the strawberries and she lost her way-"

"And found you instead?"

Dorothea smiles. "Of course, Rapunzel. As I've said, all who need my help find me. First, I had the girl help me with chores, and she neither complained nor sulked. But she was like a little lost lamb, alone and unsure of herself. It was as though she could not see what a gift she was, so I set her in the room you sleep in—and each night she became more radiant, more confident. I kept her for a week and she never asked to return home. Still, I knew that for her to find her way, she would have to face the life God had given her. I sent her away with—"

"You gave her strawberries in the middle of winter?"

"Is that so difficult to believe?"

I look around me at the comfortable but modest furnishings, table, chairs, and cupboards all made out of the forest's greenery. I stare at Dorothea and wonder if I imagine the shimmer that seems to glitter over her. Is it difficult to believe? Not after my journey thus far. "So, you gave her the strawberries she needed?"

"And a bit of enchantment to help her along . . ." The woman begins to laugh, a great bubbling laugh that shakes her whole being. "Oh, Rapunzel, each time the girl spoke, gold and jewels came from her mouth, and her appearance grew more beautiful. But when the stepsister came to my door to receive the same enchantment—well, she complained and sulked, demanded what she should never have, and so . . ." She is crying now from the hilarity of what she remembers. Her body jiggles as she struggles to get the rest of the story out. "She returned home with thorns, and each time she spoke, toads came out of her mouth."

"Dorothea!" I try to sound outraged, but I begin giggling instead.

"The enchantment would hold so long as she was selfish. If she would simply care for others, use kind words, it would have been broken . . . But alas, the last I knew, she is overcrowded with toads, and the true daughter has been rewarded with a wonderful marriage and a home full of children."

"Does she still spout gold and jewels?" I can imagine that they might get in the way after a time.

"No, dear me, no, that was only to help her father, for he owed quite a bit of money, you know. No, I daresay her life is quite ordinary now; she is quite likely a grandmother with a few children of her own left at home. I'm sure she and her husband have squabbles like anyone else; I'm sure they have difficulty when he cannot find enough meat for the table. But all in all, her life is good."

Part of me longs to reach for what Dorothea is offering, but I don't wish to be released. Not yet. I like things as they are.

◦৩৯৯৩০

LAST NIGHT my beloved shifted back to Nicholas in the middle of our embrace. I tried not to be angry—after all, Nicholas needed Matild, and I tried my best to play the part. I even heard the twins this time and was able to leave the room to care for them without breaking the spell. I didn't question it; I didn't try to will myself out. It is what Nicholas wants—and as long as my love returns on the morrow, it is what I desire as well.

SLIPPERY

Slippery. My love slides through my fingers again and again, and I cannot hold back the dawn. I feel I have gone a bit mad, but I will hold it back from coming tonight—I must! I must find a way to bind him to myself, to keep him forever. I love Dorothea, but my heart breaks now to see morning has come and Paul has gone, to hear the fire crackle and smell breakfast cooking. I hear his soft words which keep me from leaving, and I believe I am happy. But there must be a way to keep him from going so that I will no longer endure this torment.

⁂

"Child, you look a fright!" I did not respond to Dorothea's knocks and she has found me limp upon the bed. "What is wrong?"

I shake my head.

"It can't be as bad as that. Child, don't look at me with such eyes." Her old, wrinkled hands have surprising strength as they lift me and push me to get dressed. I watch them as they begin to smooth the wrinkles out of the bed. They hover over his side, I wonder if she can still feel his warmth. "Does he still come each night?"

"He only holds me!" I spit out and begin to cry, my breath sucking in and out as though I can never get enough air. "And then—then he's gone!" I am wheezing and shaking, still holding the day's clothing. I find myself staring at it as though it is poisoned.

"Oh, Rapunzel, you did not think to keep him, did you?"

But I cannot answer.

"It is not him, but his memory you hold. I thought you would have sorted this by now and moved on. It's been weeks, almost a whole season."

My eyes keep spilling and I can no longer make her out.

"Rapunzel, you have the opportunity to say goodbye. I thought that was why you came. How can we learn without memory? How can we see without recalling images of the past and the resulting change? How can we know where we are without realizing where we've been?" Her kind face scowls in pain, the crisp crinkles bunching up in concern. "I thought you would understand after we spoke, but you have clung too hard."

I blink the darkness away and, feeling less dizzy, I see the old woman wipe away her frown and smile at me. A familiar shimmer shifts in her appearance—*witch*? It couldn't be her in that sweet, wrinkled face.

She sees my question before I allow myself to ask it.

"My child, I am not a witch—and I'm certainly not *your witch*." It is a good joke, so she chuckles.

"This place . . . Nicholas, Matild, my love?"

"Not all things need explaining. This is the place of sorting, of letting go and letting be. It is not forever. Tonight you must say goodbye." Her gentle hand pats mine, but her dark little eyes pin me. "Rapunzel, you must try harder. You must beware. Do not let yourself be lost."

I dry my eyes and try to steady myself. "Dorothea, come, how do you think I could lose myself? I am myself, I am always with me." I try to laugh, but fail, knowing something darker is at work here, pulling at me to follow it, though I close my eyes to what it is. I begin to dress and then follow her down to the kitchen.

Dorothea nods at me, pouring boiling water into her clay cups and handing me one. She does not ready our meal, but motions for me to sit opposite her at the table. I feel the heat through the clay and look into the water as the small pouch colors the water with its dark brew. Her voice lilts as it picks up the thread of story where she feels she must begin.

"She was no princess, nor destined to become one. Simple, like most of us, but haunted by what she longed for."

"Then evil found her and challenged her." My sarcastic voice snaps. "She felt incapable or powerless, but she complied and was rewarded for her obedience and those who opposed her lost all they had.

"The good and well-meaning are not always rewarded. Sometimes the wicked win, Dorothea." I regret my callous words as soon as I hear them voiced. My hands wrap around the heated cup and I continue to stare into its depths.

"Dorothea, forgive me, but though I have encountered kindness since coming out into this world, I have seen such cruelty, such unfairness. Why are such things?"

"Oh, my sweet girl—the good do not always receive immediate blessings, and the wicked often prosper for a season; but would you content yourself with being wicked?"

"No, but nor do I wish to live a life where I must watch evil triumph!" A sob catches at my voice.

"Dear child, you must sort through this, you must make peace with your past. You can still love and go on living."

"What? How can I? All I have ever loved was taken from me—" I stop myself. "It doesn't matter." I turn my back on Dorothea to try to find something to do, something to do away from her to impede further conversation.

THE GHOST

*D*orothea, wise in her age, does not follow me but allows me to go about chores that could wait till later, so we skip breaking fast and set to work without talking. I sew while she rests after the silent midday meal, but I find my eyes looking into the flames often, wondering over the details of the story I interrupted. When Dorothea rises and sets about making the evening meal, I greet her with a hug. "I'm sorry for my rudeness. I have no excuse."

"Rapunzel, I know you are in pain. That is why you have come here. You must choose your way."

I know she is right, but I am content with my days and nights as they are. If I must choose another way, then it will lead me out her door, leaving behind the memories of my love forever, I fear. I am wary of leaving and long to stay. I shake my head, resigned. "Tell me the rest of the story."

"You know the rest of the story; the evil succeeds for a time and good suffers. But eventually . . . Come with me."

I follow the old woman to the back of the house where she shuffles to the door opposite mine, which I have never seen open. Though we have cleaned the entire house, this one room has remained closed, and I had thought it special, meant only for those precious visitors that she looked forward to seeing. Now, looking into her sad eyes, I know some tragedy has taken place in this room. "I have not opened this door in ever so long. For a time, I opened it daily and tried to call her back to me, but I know now it does no good. But neither can I bar the door, for one day she might choose of her own will to return."

"Who, Dorothea? What are you speaking of?"

"My child, Ysentrud. Long ago I had a child in this very room, and here she lived and played until one day she grew to be favored by a nearby farmer. He was a kind man —a bit fastidious, but we liked him well enough. Just before they were to be wed, he was killed in a horrible accident. He was stepped on by one of his animals when it became frightened. My Ysentrud retreated into this room and refused to come out again. I have been able to help many people, but never my own child."

"How long ago, Dorothea?" My voice is choked as I watch her open the door.

"Long before you were born, long before the trees that surround us were saplings. Long, long ago, she lost herself in fancies that she might find him, pretend to be with him, or some such thing." Before my eyes can adjust to the dimness of the room, the overwhelming stench of something rotting nauseates me. I close my nostrils and hasten to peer into the ghostly glow of the room and see a figure standing, spreading out its translucent arms and a warbling voice begins singing. I try to take a step back, but Dorothea nudges me forward and closes the door behind me. My breathing comes in short gasps as I turn to try to open it.

Trying to calm myself I bang on the door, "Dorothea? Let me out!"

Her voice comes through, muffled. "You must face your destiny if you continue to travel the path your feet head down."

"Dorothea?" I feel the panic climbing up inside me, fear I have not felt since Bluebeard stood over me, since I stood by, helpless, as I watched as Adeliza's child die.

The singing stops and I turn my head to look at the ghoulish woman before me. "Has she shut you in here? Have you come to grieve?" The voice is dry and raspy, her features gaunt. She has frightfully white skin stretched taut over malnourished bones with a threadbare nightdress that does nothing to conceal the body it can no longer cover. Her rheumy eyes do not look at me but stare glazed in front of her, stringy hair hanging limply in front of her face. "I have many songs of mourning we can sing together if you would like. It has been so long since anyone joined me in my songs."

I swallow to whisper, "How have I not heard you in all these weeks?"

"No one hears me unless they wish to. I am the living dead—I cannot let go of life and I cannot stop mourning."

My whole body is trembling, and I can't seem to make it stop. "Why won't you come out?"

"I cannot, not until my time of mourning passes. Have you never loved someone so much that you could not exist without them? I cannot live without my love."

Her mouth is a black hollow, and when she speaks I see that all of her teeth have rotted and several fallen out. How can one girl continue to exist this way? Why does Dorothea allow her to?

"Can you not try to find your way out? Can you not try for your mother's sake?"

"I have only love for the death that will release me to be with my love."

"Have you been cursed, forced to live this way?"

Her grey eyes find me through their haze, her stringy hair now moving as she jerks her head around to me. "Don't you think I could have chosen this life for myself?" She laughs, a mirthless sound. "This is no life, but one day my debt to my love will be paid." Then her mournful warble begins again and she reaches out to clutch my arm. "Sing with me." She breathes her foul breath at me, and I turn to beat on the door. "Sing with me!" I pound louder, and the door bursts open. I fall into Dorothea's arms and we cry together as she shuts the door.

We go back to the kitchen and weep as we drink our tepid drinks. She turns to me. "Rapunzel, you left behind your tower. Don't return to it."

LIVING

he evening drags on with dreary steps, each one taking me closer to the night I dread. My heart has withered into a puckered prune, hopeless. I am not angry at Dorothea, though; I know she is right. I could feel myself slipping, wanting to join Nicholas in his pretense forever. Perhaps I would have become a mirror image of Ysentrud.

As I ready myself for bed, I begin to sing. Even before I have reached the bed, my beloved embraces me from behind and I smile. I breathe in his scent and reach back with my right hand to him. I touch his cheek and then dig my fingers into his uncovered hair. I am tempted to stay here, to give myself to this wondrous phantom. But I mustn't. I know now that I will be forever lost if I allow myself the indulgence. If I lose myself, who will find me?

He turns me into himself and I bury my head in his chest. All at once I know I must say goodbye. A terror grips my heart—if I even allow myself another moment, even for a kiss, all will be lost.

"Goodbye," I whisper. His hands, now Nicholas's hands, tear at my short hair and pull my head back to stare into his eyes. The candle's light and shadows play across his face.

"What did you say?" He spits and I now see a white scar cutting across his left brow down the bridge of his nose to his right cheek. My eyes scan the room, Dorothea's room, none of our pretense left. His grip on me is fading, and his voice is desperate.

"I said 'goodbye'."

"You can't leave." His form and voice change once again to resemble my love; the appearance of the room quivers but cannot transform all the way. "I love you, Rapunzel—stay with me." Paul's image leans down to kiss me.

I will no longer allow myself to become entangled with his charade. I just close my eyes.

When I open them again, the candle is out, and the room is colder. But though my heart hurts, I know it is time to go to bed, alone.

❧

MORNING'S COME, and I rise to meet it by myself. I gather my things, the new clothes Dorothea has insisted I take with me in a beautiful, sturdy bag of tooled leather. I brush my short hair, then mask it once more with my wimple.

As I take my leave, the old woman smiles at me.

My words are stuck; I have no idea how to thank her. I want her to tell me I'm better; after last night, I will be well now.

"You have a door. Why are you still here?" She turns from me to return to her day's work. I suppose she is preparing for her visitors, perhaps people like me, or maybe her family whom she loves and has missed.

Her question sticks me like a thorn as I turn without an embrace to walk away. My foot is at once enveloped in a mist and the cloud rises to engulf my entire being. I am walking into the unknown, but that is no different than anything else I have done since leaving my tower.

I close my eyes and take two slow steps. I have to blink my eyes once again at the bright light that seeps through my lids. I am not in a dark, oppressive wood, but at the entry of some great city set in a valley between two towering mountains. Before me is a horse's head hanging on a wooden city gate. Much to my amazement and shock, his eyes open and he smiles at me.

"Good lady, you have come to the right city. Take your place and serve my mistress well."

My mouth remains open, my mind half-wondering where the oppressive, dark wood has gone, and the other what a beheaded horse can have to say to me. How can he say anything? My mouth is still open when I suddenly shut it up and accidentally bite my tongue hard. Talking felines, horse heads, all made of the same magic. I swallow the taste of blood. I need to develop some shield to protect me from this naïve shock.

I collect myself to say calmly, "Who is your mistress and where might I find her? I am in search of employment."

The horse whinnies his assent. "I am Falada." He gives the distinct impression he is bowing to me, though he lacks the front legs to do it properly. "My mistress is the former goose-girl, the present queen, and you should find her at court."

I laugh heartily at the strange creature. "I am but a common maid—they would not allow me at court."

A different voice answers, "You are anything but common, and I am quite sure they will find you of utmost necessity once they realize who you are, Rapunzel."

I see a flick of a tail in front of me as the gate opens outward—Falada and my mischievous cat have become acquainted, it would seem!

"Come along, now!" She opens her mouth to yawn, showing white pointed teeth. "We haven't all day, and we certainly need to begin working out this puzzle. Besides, though I love Dorothea dearly, there is more to your story than even she could imagine."

⊱⊰

Want More Now?

"She cannot begin at the beginning," my cat purrs.
"She was not there at the beginning."

Would you like to begin at the beginning?

As my gift to you, I would like to send you a copy of the novella *Before the Tower* so you might see for yourself the story of two sisters, their struggle to survive, and their choices that led Rapunzel to life imprisoned in a tower.

Get it here: dl.bookfunnel.com/wftepfzx96

Amidst the Castles **available now!**

A VENGEFUL WITCH. A controlling prince. Will Rapunzel find her way?

As Rapunzel resumes her journey, she doesn't realize she will be pulled into more fairytale mysteries. Who is the troubadour and why is he convinced they must be together? Is Cat actually a woman, and if so, why was she transformed? Why won't the witch relinquish her hold on Rapunzel?

But greater than these questions remains the mystery of what she should do with her life and whom she should spend it with.

Find *Amidst the Castles* at your store of choice:
authorjroe.com/book/amidst

GLOSSARY

Chemise – a slip-like gown that was worn as the first layer of dress for women in Rapunzel's world. It would be naturally colored, typically an off-white color. Often, this was worn as a nightgown at night when the other layers of dress would be removed.

Cotehardie – a fitted gown worn over the chemise with sleeves cut to various lengths according to station in Rapunzel's world. The higher the station, the more intricate the sleeves, sometimes tight at the elbows and bell-shaped at the wrist or short at the elbows with a streaming tail called a tippet. The bottom of the cotehardie might also be lined with fur to show off the station of a woman.

Liripipe – a long tail that extended from the hood that men of the Northlands and Alleria in Rapunzel's world enjoyed wearing to cover their heads. Often this tail was wrapped around the head and, like all of a man's clothing, would coordinate with his lord's colors if he served in a castle.

Surcoat – the outermost layer of dress a woman would wear in Rapunzel's world, over which she would wear a cloak to go outdoors in cool weather. The gown was sideless and would complement the cotehardie's coloring, often cut a bit short if the cotehardie beneath had a fur-lined hem. The surcoat was frequently embellished with embroidery.

Wimple - a piece of delicate white linen wrapped beneath the neck and often worn by married women in Rapunzel's time to cover their hair.

DON'T CARRY YOUR PRISON WITH YOU

1. Rapunzel's life was dominated by the imprisonment inflicted by the witch. How did this shape her?

2. Do you relate to Rapunzel's sense of isolation, or do you feel like your life is a journey with others?

3. Rapunzel is greatly affected by the friendships she forms, but because of her isolation early in life she has a very difficult time staying in one place and sharing herself with others. How does this affect her relationships?

4. Do you have anything in your life that makes it difficult for you to build relationships and trust people?

5. Rapunzel clearly understands sin; she states it is "action or inaction": *a man stealing or refusing to provide, a woman lying or unwilling to love, a child hitting or not obeying.* Do you agree? What sin do

you see in your own life that you can't seem to stop?

6. Rapunzel is told during her time caring for Adeliza that Jesus, the Son of God, came to earth because of His great love for mankind to set them free from their sins. She struggles with the idea of someone perfect dying for her sins; do you relate to her struggle?

7. Have you ever personally accepted this sacrifice?

8. Rapunzel ponders the idea of a cloistered life, not wishing to judge those sitting inside praying and cleaning, but she instinctively feels faith requires going forth to find needs and meet them. What do you believe about this? *(For more information about the duty of Christians in serving, see James 2:14-17 and 1 John 3:17-18.)*

9. Rapunzel wants *"a place to belong, a people to call my own, to live with, love, and serve."* Do you have those things?

10. Have you suffered a loss like Adeliza? If so, how did you react?

11. If you have faith in the God of the Bible, were you able to see God's hand at work during your own tragedy? After your tragedy? (For more understanding of how God uses His Spirit and love to care for those He loves, read Romans 8:26-39.)

12. How does Adeliza's response to her tragedy affect Rapunzel?

13. Adeliza gives every indication of living a life of

faith by placing her trust in the unseen God of the Bible, "Now faith is the assurance of things hoped for, the conviction of things not seen."* How does Adeliza's faith in God's goodness carry her through this difficult season? (*Hebrews 11:1 ESV. See also the rest of Hebrews 11 for more inspiring references of faith.)

14. Why do you think it seemed to repel Rapunzel?

15. Rapunzel struggles throughout the book with the loss of her first true friend and love, Paul. Have you ever lost anyone you love? How do you think grief should be processed?

16. Do you agree with Rapunzel's desire to stay at Dorothea's? Would you rather live in a world of make-believe where you can pretend what went wrong never happened, or the real world where you have to accept loss and find a way to keep going?

17. What adventures do you think Cat is about to pull Rapunzel into? What adventures do you foresee coming in your own life?

ACKNOWLEDGMENTS

It has occurred to me, as I have worked on publishing this first book in the Journey Series, how very alone Rapunzel believes herself to be. This has made me ever so grateful that I am not.

Thank you first and foremost to the God of heaven and earth who saved me from eternal separation from Him. May He always be glorified above all else.

Thank you to my husband and children for helping me dream big dreams. Jeff, I love you; Katie, Sydney, and Caleb, I am so honored to be your mom. Thank you to my parents for encouraging me though I wore you out by telling you stories. Thank you to my sisters for listening. Thank you to Margaret and my new sisters for joining our crazy family. Thank you to Kelly and Rachel, Bob and Margie for being my second family and always loving me. Thank you to Gwynn for so faithfully holding me up in prayer. Thank you to Jody for editing, encouraging, and helping my dreams come true. Thank you to Lauren, Heather, and Kevin for believing this was possible and teaching me to laugh so hard. Thank you to Sara and Mandy for praying and offering hilarious words of wisdom. Thank you to David and Cindy for speaking truth. Thank you to my entire Saint Jo family, especially Candice, Leigh, Ruth, Linda, and Tiffani whose friendship has meant so much. Thank you to Aunt Celia and Uncle Doug for adopting us when we moved. Thank you to Heather, Mike, Josh, Travis, and Sean for inspiring me to write again even though you didn't know it. Thank you to Amie, Kristen, Allison, and Abby for helping me find a better way to tell the story.

Finally, thank you to all who are joining Rapunzel on her journey. May we all learn and continue to grow.

ABOUT THE AUTHOR

A lover of books and fairytales, JacQueline uses her faith and life experience with chronic pain/depression to discover new ways of telling old stories as well as her own. She lives in North Alabama with her amazing karate husband and three book-crazy children. She takes every opportunity to drink coffee while wearing dangly earrings and the color purple. Join her newsletter when you download your free copy of *Before the Tower* by visiting dl.bookfunnel.com/wftepfzx96.

Find JacQueline at AuthorJRoe.com, and you can also follow her on social media:

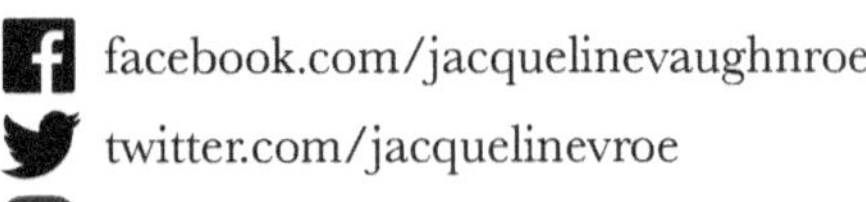